T0031509

VISUAL TIMELINES SCIENCE

INVENTIONS AND DISCOVERIES YEAR BY YEAR

ANNE ROONEY

ILLUSTRATED BY VIOLET TOBACCO

ARCTURUS

WHO'S ON THE COVER?

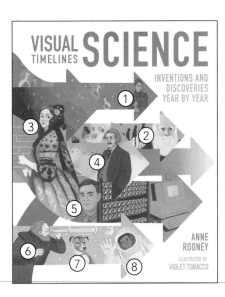

These are the remarkable scientists on the cover, and a list of pages where you can find more information about them.

1 Marie Curie, page 83

2 Charles Darwin, pages 76, 79, 80, 81, 100, and 101

3 Ada Lovelace, pages 75 and 112

4 Albert Einstein, pages 76, 88, 89, 90, and 103

5 Alan Turing, page 97

6 Galileo Galilei, pages 59, 61, 63, and 64

7 Strelka, page 104

8 Mae Jemison, page 117

ARCTURUS

This edition published in 2022 by Arcturus Publishing Limited
26/27 Bickels Yard, 151–153 Bermondsey Street,
London SE1 3HA

Copyright © Arcturus Holdings Limited

All rights reserved. No part of this publication may be reproduced, stored in a retrieval system, or transmitted, in any form or by any means, electronic, mechanical, photocopying, recording or otherwise, without prior written permission in accordance with the provisions of the Copyright Act 1956 (as amended). Any person or persons who do any unauthorised act in relation to this publication may be liable to criminal prosecution and civil claims for damages.

Author: Anne Rooney
Illustrator: Violet Tobacco
Designer: Ms Mousepenny
Editors: Felicity Forster and Becca Clunes
Design Manager: Jessica Holliland
Managing Editor: Joe Harris

ISBN: 978-1-3988-2022-7
CH010048US
Supplier 29, Date 1122, PI 00001968

Printed in China

CONTENTS

INTRODUCTION

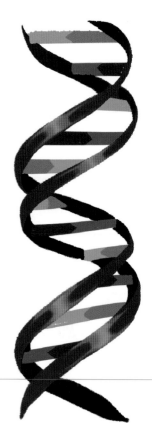

Science explains how the universe works. Through it, we are slowly discovering the set of rules that everything in the universe follows. These rules explain why planets stay in orbit, how plants grow, and how different chemicals react together. Humans are the only animals to have developed science. It is an inquisitive approach to the world that looks for explanations and uses the things around us in new ways.

Science is more than a set of experiments and observations like those you might do at school or that a scientist might do in a laboratory. It's an attitude and a way of looking at the world that leads us to notice what happens around us. It makes us look for explanations, for causes and effects.

Modern technology connects us to the world

DNA provides the genetic instructions necessary for all living things

How? Why? What if?

These are questions people have asked about the world for thousands of years—and possibly hundreds of thousands of years! Wondering about the natural world and investigating it has given us the chance to develop everything from simple stone tools to spacecraft, vaccines, and phones. These questions—how? why? what if?—lie at the heart of science.

The thermoscope was an early type of thermometer

Isaac Newton recognized that white light is made up of a spectrum

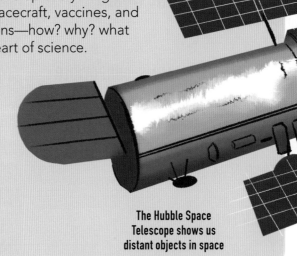

The Hubble Space Telescope shows us distant objects in space

Stories of science

Our early ancestors paid attention to events, such as earthquakes, and objects, such as the stars, and tried to explain them. Many explanations were pure invention with no evidence to suggest they were true. For example, some people believed that earthquakes are caused by a dragon or some other creature deep below the ground moving around, or that stars are the spirits of heroes placed in the sky by gods.

Starting around 2,500 years ago in Ancient Greece, people began to search for a different kind of explanation, given in terms of real observations rather than exciting stories. These first attempts at scientific explanation were not always right, and often not even based on evidence, but they were based in the real world. They could suggest that the stars are burning rocks, for example, because rocks and fire exist, and most things, when heated enough, will burn.

Ancient Armenians thought that the Milky Way was straw dropped by a mythical king

We now know volcanic eruptions are not caused by angry gods

Science through time

Science builds on previous discoveries. It tries paths of exploration that might be wrong, and it changes when new evidence comes along. Being scientific means being open to change, to revising or even throwing away old ideas if they don't fit with new discoveries.

Humans began the scientific processes of observing, recording, explaining, and using the world around them before they recognized an idea of "science." Our early ancestors used fire to change materials and to produce heat. They began to work with materials such as stone, bone, and metals. This doesn't sound like science, but even to make a stone spearhead they had to notice, observe, remember, and use the ways in which stone naturally breaks.

Smelting liquid copper

Wooden shaft with a stone spearhead

5

Ancient Greeks suggested that the Sun is a nearby star nearly 2,500 years ago

World of science

Scientific discoveries have been made all around the world at different times. At some times, people in one region did more scientific work than people in others. Five thousand years ago, people in the Middle East and the area that is now Pakistan were leading the way. China was at the heart of scientific discoveries 2,000 years ago. Europe had the most scientific developments from around 1500–1900.

When one area has moved more quickly than others, that's often been because there were particular needs or particular resources in that area. People find ways to solve problems, and that often involves science. If they have free time and resources, they might turn to science to explore the world around them, too. Now, science is a truly global project with international teams from countries all around the world working together on important questions.

An early Chinese seismoscope for detecting earthquakes

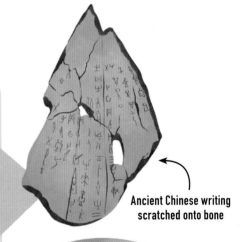

Ancient Chinese writing scratched onto bone

Making it personal

We can't link the developments made long ago to individuals. We don't know who first hardened wooden spears in a fire or turned clay on a wheel to make pots more quickly. Many developments appeared again and again in different places. Regions separated by uncrossable oceans saw the same developments, such as farming crops and making beads, so these must have been discovered more than once.

After people developed writing, they sometimes recorded who made a discovery. For the last thousand years, we often have names associated with discoveries. We know that Shen Kuo in China wrote about climate change in 1080, and that Antonie van Leeuwenhoek was the first person to see bacteria through a microscope in Holland in 1683. More recently, scientists have often worked together in large teams. That's why we can't name a single person responsible for putting a spacecraft on Mars, for example.

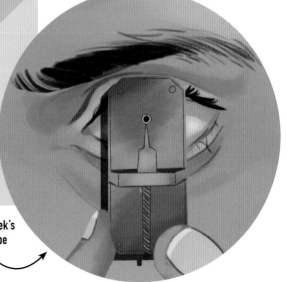

Leeuwenhoek's microscope

Science lost to history

The timelines in this book highlight some of the most important and interesting scientific developments over all human history. We know most about discoveries made in cultures where people had a written language and could record their findings. From times before writing, we know the most from cultures that left works of art made in lasting materials. The people in these societies were not more advanced or clever than others. Many people who lived in groups that left no records probably also made important discoveries, but we know nothing of them. We know, for example, that the people of Micronesia were the most skilled navigators in the world, understanding all about the tides, winds, and currents of the sea. But their knowledge was passed on by word of mouth, and even today their maps are not lasting, but are made by laying out shells in the sand and drawing lines between them. This type of science leaves no record except in the minds of the people who discover or inherit it.

There are undoubtedly gaps in our timeline, but we don't even know where they are.

Humans began creating art by making handprints on cave walls

Ancient Egyptians split reeds to make papyrus for writing on

Science has led us to figure out what killed the dinosaurs millions of years ago

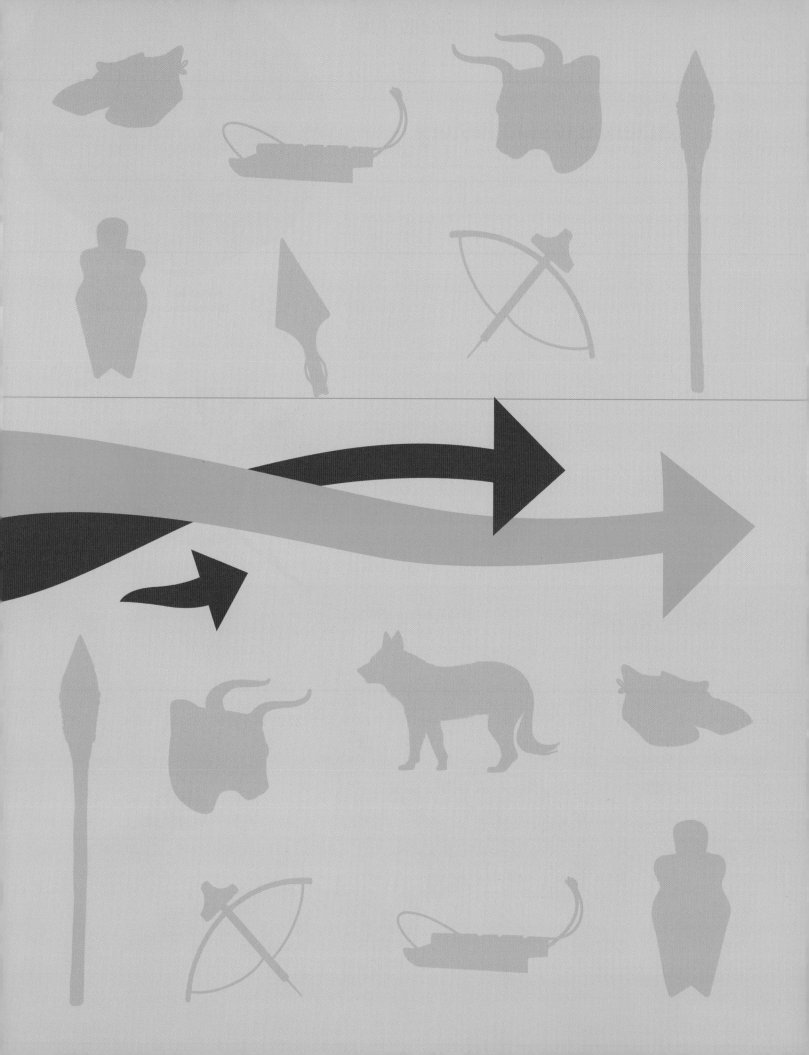

CHAPTER 1

FIRST THINGS

A scene of everyday life in the Stone Age doesn't look as though it involved much science. But humans were already making use of the properties of materials, changing them through fire, and shaping them. They were using furs and insulation to keep warm. They were mixing chemical pigments to make paints to decorate their walls and their bodies.

We can't know whether they had any kind of scientific ideas, but we do know that they had scientific practices. Their application of scientific processes set early humans apart from other animals. It also put them on the path toward shaping the world.

Some of the events in this chapter happened a very long time ago. They are given dates in the form of millions or thousands of years ago (counting backward from now). From 12,000 years ago, dates are given the labels BCE (Before Common Era) or CE (Common Era). The Common Era started around 2,000 years ago—it's where we count our current dates from. The date 10,000 BCE is 12,000 years ago.

2.6 MILLION–100,000 YEARS AGO

Humankind's earliest type of activity that used scientific knowledge was toolmaking. Knowledge about materials and their properties enabled our ancestors to make and use the tools that started humankind's journey to the modern world.

2.6 MILLION YEARS AGO

Long before the evolution of modern humans, early hominins (types of human) began using **pebble tools**. They chipped flakes off a flint pebble to give a sharp edge, and they used this for scraping, pounding, and chopping.

800,000 YEARS AGO

People made **rafts** from bamboo or wood, and they used these to cross the sea from Bali to the island of Flores.

Bamboo poles lashed together to make a raft

780,000 YEARS AGO

Early humans in Spain used **furs** to keep warm, but did not stitch them into clothes. With furs, they could go into places much colder than they could tolerate without coverings.

2.6 MILLION YEARS AGO

Stone hand axes were used to scrape an animal's skin

1.7 MILLION YEARS AGO

The first type of true human—*Homo erectus*—made teardrop-shaped hand **axes** by carefully chipping flint from several sides of a stone.

1.5 MILLION–790,000 YEARS AGO

People first used **fire** in a hearth inside a cave. It is possible that they captured fires started naturally by lightning before they made their own fires. They improved their tools and weapons by treating them with fire, and also used fire to cook their food. Better food led to humans having larger brains, and keeping warm helped them survive in colder areas. Sitting around the fire also increased social activity and maybe the use of language.

600,000 YEARS AGO

People in Germany used sharpened sticks as **spears**.

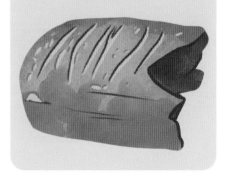

One of the momentous developments made by humankind was using language to communicate. This might have begun as early as 200,000 years ago or perhaps as late as 60,000 years ago.

500,000 YEARS AGO

The earliest evidence of a **shelter** that was built rather than found (like a cave) is post holes left from two huts or shelters made of branches and sticks in Japan.

Shelter made from saplings and stones

200,000 YEARS AGO

People used sticky juice from birch trees as **glue**. This is soft when warm, but turns solid as it cools.

100,000 YEARS AGO

200,000 YEARS AGO

The earliest known **bedding** consists of piles of grass preserved in South Africa. The remains lie on ash, probably indicating that people burned their old bedding and laid new grass over it.

500,000 YEARS AGO

Our early ancestors in Africa began to use **stone spearheads**. This meant that they could hunt more efficiently, killing large animals and thereby gaining a better diet. This probably improved humans' growth and bone development.

Stone spearhead attached to a wooden shaft with twine made from plants or leather

170,000 YEARS AGO

People probably started wearing **clothes**, perhaps made of simple animal hides. Although no clothes have survived, the body louse, which lives in clothes, evolved at this time.

120,000 YEARS AGO

A bone carved with six lines found in Israel is the earliest evidence of meaningful **mark-making** by an early human, although its meaning is not known.

100,000–12,000 YEARS AGO (10,000 BCE)

The achievements of early people were not limited to our own ancestors, early *Homo sapiens*. Other types of early humans probably also made art, tools, and perhaps clothing. But by 40,000 years ago, *Homo sapiens* was the only surviving species of human.

100,000–70,000 YEARS AGO

Using ocher, a kind of clay containing minerals, people in South Africa made red, orange, and yellow **pigments** for painting on cave walls and probably their own bodies.

Handprints on a cave wall

40,000–27,500 YEARS AGO

Evidence from ancient toe bones suggests that people started to wear **shoes** long before the oldest surviving shoes were made. The oldest known shoe is 9–10,000 years old, made of sagebrush bark, and was found in Oregon, USA.

100,000 YEARS AGO

72,000–61,000 YEARS AGO

Surviving stone arrowheads show that people in South Africa made a **bow** for firing **arrows** at the animals they hunted. Some arrows might have been tipped with poison. If so, people knew which plants produce poison and how to prepare it— some simple chemistry.

50,000 YEARS AGO

Sewing needles found in Siberia, Russia, are evidence of **stitching,** probably to make clothes. It's not known what was used for making the clothes—perhaps animal skins.

72,000 YEARS AGO

The first **lamps** were made from shells or hollow rocks. They were stuffed with moss soaked in animal fat, which burned easily.

44,000–43,000 YEARS AGO

The oldest surviving **measuring device** was found in Eswatini and is made from the leg bone of a baboon. It has 29 notches and might have been used to count the phases of the Moon or record a woman's menstrual cycle.

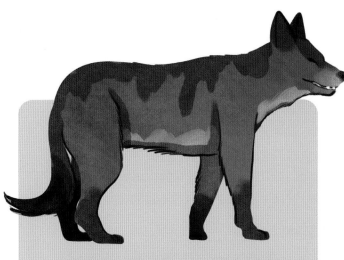

40,000–30,000 YEARS AGO

The first domesticated **dogs**, descended from wolves, were trapped and kept by humans as hunting companions (see page 15).

17,300 YEARS AGO

Cave paintings in Lascaux, France, seem to show constellations of stars, such as the Pleiades and Hyades. This is the first evidence of interest in **astronomy**.

20,000 YEARS AGO

The oldest fragments of clay **containers, cooking pots, plates, and cups** come from China.

14,000 YEARS AGO

A young man who died 14,000 years ago in Italy had a cavity in a tooth that had been partly cleaned of rotten matter using a flint tool. He is the earliest known **dental patient**.

12,000 YEARS AGO

29,000–25,000 YEARS AGO

Clay was discovered and used around the world. A naturally occurring type of soil, it can be mixed with water, shaped, and dried to become hard. It becomes a ceramic if fired in an oven or fire and is even harder. The "Venus of Dolní Věstonice," found in the Czech Republic, is the oldest piece of ceramic art.

14,000 YEARS AGO

The earliest known **dried food** is fish dried in the sun in Egypt. The technique has been used around the world to preserve food.

30,000 YEARS AGO

Flax was spun and dyed in Georgia and made into threads or cord for fixing spearheads to spears, and also for making baskets and clothes.

Other types of early humans—Neanderthals in Europe and Denisovans in Asia—died out, leaving modern humans, *Homo sapiens*, the only survivors by around 40,000 years ago.

DOWN ON THE FARM

For hundreds of thousands of years, people lived as hunter-gatherers, finding food where they could by hunting, fishing, and collecting fruit, nuts, seeds, roots, and leaves. That all changed around 12,000 years ago with the Neolithic Revolution, when people began to settle in one place and farm the land. The world warmed as the last glacial period (Ice Age) ended. Ice and snow that covered northern parts of America, Europe, and Asia melted, and sea levels rose. With the change in climate, people settled and took up farming.

SHAPING PLANTS AND ANIMALS

Within a short time, people began to change the characteristics of plants and animals. They did this by choosing to breed from the "best," such as the fattest sheep, or to collect and grow seeds from the plants that gave the most or tastiest foods. Although early farmers didn't know how plants and animals inherited their features, trial and error gave them improved crops and animals.

Making the banana

The earliest **crop plants** grown in the Middle East from around 11,500 years ago included wheat, barley, peas, lentils, and chickpeas (also known as garbanzo beans). In other parts of the world, people grew different crops, including sugar cane in New Guinea (9,000 years ago) and sweet potatoes, cocoa, and bananas in South America (10,000–7,000 years ago). Comparing a modern and wild banana shows how much difference selective breeding has made over just a few thousand years.

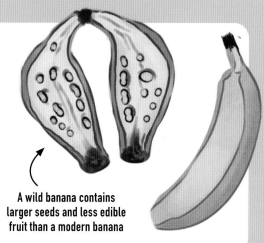

A wild banana contains larger seeds and less edible fruit than a modern banana

Farm animals

People kept **animals** for a steady supply of food. Animal bodies also provided leather or fur, bones for making needles and weapons, and tallow (fat) for lamps or candles. In the Middle East, people began to keep mouflon (a kind of wild sheep), then goats.

At first, herders had a nomadic lifestyle, moving with their animals to areas of fresh grass. From around 9,000 years ago, settled communities kept other animals, such as pigs and cattle.

Early farmers began to make changes to the animals they kept. Around 7,500 years ago, altering the breeding period of some animals resulted in a year-round milk supply.

An aurochs, a type of ancient cow

A mouflon, belived to be the ancestor of all modern sheep

BEST FRIENDS

The first animals that people changed were **wolves**, even before farming began. The footprints of a child walking alongside a wolf 30,000 years ago are the earliest signs of a companion animal. By 28,500 years ago, the bones of wolves and dogs were already different. The first wolf-dogs were probably companions and helpers in hunting. With wolves, people could hunt large animals, and the wolves were rewarded with a steady supply of food and somewhere warm to live. People probably bred from and kept those that had the features they preferred, maybe including friendliness. This slowly changed them into domestic dogs.

**Neolithic shepherd
and his wolf-dog**

10,000–6000 BCE

Around 12,000 years ago, as people started to settle and farm the land, there is better datable evidence of human activities. We change from talking about "years ago" to giving dates, starting with 10,000 BCE.

10,000 BCE

The earliest **baskets** come from Egypt. To make baskets from twisted and woven strands of plant material, people needed to know the properties of the plants they were using and also some mathematics, thinking in three dimensions.

8000 BCE

The oldest structure made as an **astronomical calendar** is at Warren Field in Scotland. Twelve pits are arranged in an arc, and the sixth pit lines up with sunrise on the winter solstice (shortest day). This shows that people carefully tracked the movement of the Sun across the sky, as well as having cooperated in a civil engineering project.

7000 BCE

Wooden **sleds**, perhaps pulled by dogs, were used to move heavy loads over ice and snow in northern Europe. From 2700 BCE, people used sleds to transport blocks of stone over the sand in Egypt.

10,000 BCE

9000 BCE

Bricks were the first manufactured building material. They were made from mud shaped into blocks and dried in the sun in Syria and Turkey. The Sumerians (in modern-day Iraq) were the first to mass-produce bricks and use them to build their cities.

8700 BCE

People began working lumps of **copper** that they found in Bulgaria and the Middle East (see page 20).

7000 BCE

Wine made from fruit appeared independently around the world, but the earliest known wine was from China. Wine-making uses the fermenting activity of yeast.

8000 BCE

The oldest dugout **canoes** were made soon after the tools to build them were developed. Constructing a canoe like this required knowledge of wood's properties and buoyancy (its ability to float). The oldest surviving canoe is from Holland.

Wooden canoe made by hollowing out a tree trunk

7000–5500 BCE

The first people to **drill into human teeth** to clean and fix dental caries (tooth decay) lived in the Indus valley in Pakistan.

Irrigation channel carrying water from a river to crops

6000 BCE

Crop plants produce more food if they are watered generously. People in Iran and later Mesopotamia began diverting and directing river water to their crops, making **canals, dams, and gates** to control the flow.

6000 BCE

6500–6000 BCE

Waterproofing for ships and buckets was developed in Mesopotamia using bitumen. This is a sticky, thick, black form of gasoline (petrol) that was collected where it seeped from rocks.

Hole made in the back of the skull

6500 BCE

A simple but horrifying surgical procedure called **"trephining"** or **"trepanning"** consisted of making a hole in the skull with a drill or by scraping through the bone. It started independently all around the world and was probably used to treat headaches, epilepsy, and head injuries—and perhaps drive out evil spirits. Holes with healed edges show that some people survived, and some even had the operation several times.

Domesticated sheep first had a short, rough coat and were probably kept for meat and milk. But around 6000 BCE, they began to be bred for a woolly coat—a very different way of thinking about domesticated animals.

6000–4000 BCE

The invention of the wheel, which came in this period, is one of the most important early developments. In Africa, Europe, and Asia, it was revolutionary—but in South America, where there were no animals suitable for pulling carts and farm equipment, wheels appeared only on children's toys.

6000–5000 BCE

The earliest type of **plow** (sometimes spelled "plough"), called an ard plow, was made of wood, starting in Mesopotamia. A plow cuts a groove in the soil into which seeds can be planted in a straight row. It made planting quicker and more efficient.

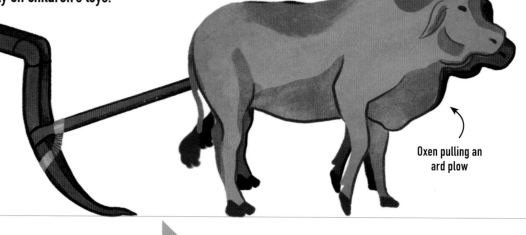

Oxen pulling an ard plow

6000 BCE

5500–5000 BCE

Metal smelting began in Serbia, with **copper** being the first metal that was extracted (see page 20).

5000 BCE

People in South America and Egypt began preserving bodies by **mummification**. The body was dried, and chemicals were used to keep it from rotting, then it was wrapped in fabric.

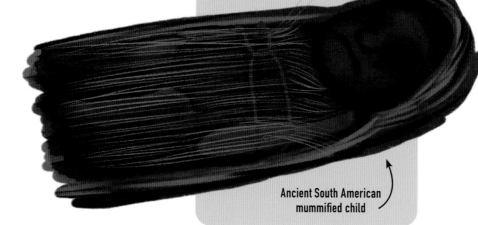

Ancient South American mummified child

5000 BCE

A Sumerian text attributed toothache to "tooth worms." It's wrong, but it shows an attempt to find a **scientific explanation** for an ailment rather than blaming it on a spirit or demon. Cures for the pain caused by tooth worms were recorded later. They included incantations (repeating spells) and mixtures of herbs, oil, and beer.

4900 BCE

The Goseck Circle in Germany is a ring of wooden stakes. It was probably built to track the rising and setting of the Sun and measure a year. An accurate **calendar** is important for farming, helping people to plan planting and harvesting, and to know when to expect events such as seasonal rains, floods, and storms.

4500 BCE

The **potter's wheel** was invented in Mesopotamia. This was a single wheel mounted on a vertical axle, used to turn a lump of clay that a potter shaped as it turned. By turning the wheel, the potter could easily make a pot symmetrical. It was the first step toward industrialization, which uses machinery to make a manufacturing task quicker and easier. It meant that pottery could be quickly mass-produced. Wheels were also used for grinding seeds such as wheat, and for moving water to irrigate crops—but not yet for vehicles.

Mesopotamian craftsman making a pot on a potter's wheel

4000 BCE

4500 BCE

People in Serbia began to mix tin into molten copper, making **bronze**.

4200—4000 BCE

The **wheel** left the potter's workshop to be adapted for transportation, with animals such as oxen, donkeys, and horses pulling carts or wagons, perhaps starting in Poland, Ukraine, or the Middle East. For a wheel to turn effectively, it must rotate freely on an axle thin enough to reduce friction but thick enough to bear a load. Cutting circular wheels and well-fitting axles needed metal tools, so metalworking must have come before the wheel. Miniature clay wheels dating from 4000 BCE are the earliest evidence of wheels.

A massive wagon with two pairs of wooden wheels that got stuck in mud in Switzerland around 3000 BCE

WORKING WITH METAL

Stone Age people fashioned tools from bone, stone, and wood with great skill, but these materials had limitations. The start of metalworking brought a great leap in the development of human societies. Metal axes, knives, and farm tools were sharper and stronger than tools made of wood and bone.

COLD COPPER

The first metals used were those that could be found as lumps, including **gold** and **copper**. These were soft enough to be shaped by hammering when cold. Copper was chosen for blades and other tools used in hunting and farming. It was hammered into sheets, which were then divided to make blades, arrowheads, choppers, and axes. The blades and arrowheads were attached to bone or wooden shafts.

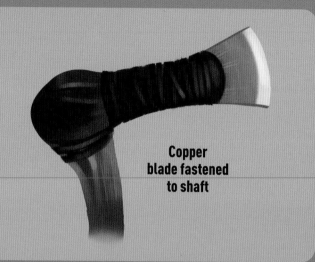

Copper blade fastened to shaft

MELTING AND SMELTING

When people were able to make hot enough fires, they began to melt copper, then pour it into shaped containers made from sand or clay, where it hardened into the form of the cavity. More detailed and complex shapes could be made this way than by hammering.

Much copper is found mixed into rock, rather than as lumps. This is called "ore." Around 5500–5000 BCE, people in eastern Europe discovered that copper could be separated from ore by heating it until the metal melted. The impurities floated to the surface and could be scooped off. This process is called "smelting."

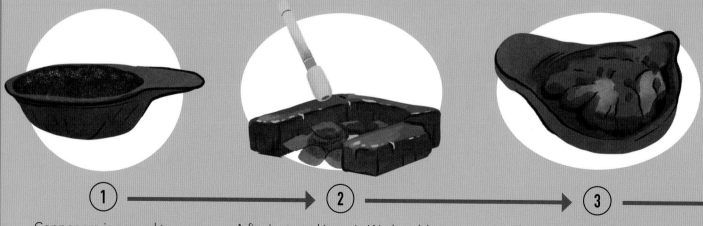

1. Copper ore is ground to small pieces and put into a clay crucible.

2. A fire is started in a pit. Workers blow extra air into it through a clay-tipped bamboo or wooden pipe to raise the temperature. The clay protects the pipe, so that it doesn't catch fire.

3. The copper melts and sinks to the bottom. The waste material floats to the top and can be scooped off and thrown away.

METAL FROM THE SKY

Iron is not found in its pure form on Earth and melts at too high a temperature for early metalworkers to have been able to smelt it. But occasionally, people found iron meteorites (rocks from space) and cold-hammered them into objects. Meteoric iron is rare, so it was probably used for special objects. A dagger buried in the tomb of the Egyptian pharaoh Tutankhamen is made of meteoric iron.

Iron meteorite

Tutankhamen's dagger

④

The liquid copper is poured into a shaped container to harden.

METAL MIXTURES

About 1,000 years after people began to smelt copper, they learned to make **bronze** (around 4500 BCE). Bronze is an "alloy"—a mixture of metals or of a metal with another substance. It is harder than copper and was made by mixing copper with lead or tin. The Bronze Age began at different times around the world and was the next great step in human development.

Bronze spearhead

4000–3000 BCE

People began to live lives that we would recognize now, many of them living in the first cities and having specialized jobs, rather than all growing their own food and making their own clothes. This led to more and more scientific advances.

3500 BCE

The Sumerians extracted oils from herbs or flowers mashed up in water to produce **medicines and perfumes**. They did this by distillation: heating a liquid until it boils and collecting the cooling vapor. When an oil or alcohol boils at a lower temperature than water, it evaporates first and can be condensed (cooled to return to a liquid) before the water boils.

Rock roses were used to make ancient remedies

4000 BCE

Metalworkers in China began to make **brass**, a mixture of copper and zinc.

4000 BCE

Fired bricks—those baked in a kiln or oven—began to replace sun-dried bricks. They were stronger, longer lasting, and could soak up heat in the daytime and give it out again at night.

4000 BCE

4000–3000 BCE

Silk was produced by unwinding the cocoon of the silkworm caterpillar and weaving the long threads into fabric. Silk may have been used earlier, perhaps 6500 BCE, but the oldest surviving silk is from around 3600 BCE.

3500 BCE

Horses were first trapped and domesticated for meat and milk in Kazakhstan, but became a means of transportation around 5,000 years ago. Donkeys were tamed in Egypt around the same time. Horses greatly increased the speed at which people could move and the distance they could easily travel. The next large increase in speed and range came with the invention of the steam engine more than 5,000 years later.

4000–3000 BCE

Wooden bow drills with a hard bit were used for drilling the semiprecious stone lapis lazuli, and in dentistry in the Indus Valley, for drilling teeth.

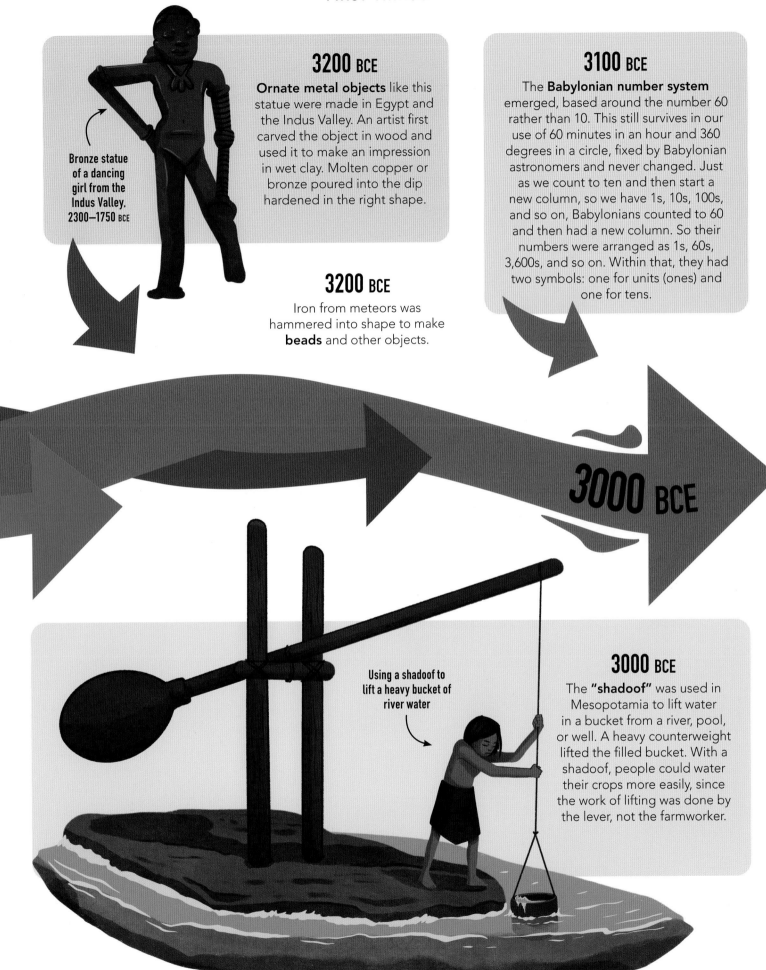

Bronze statue of a dancing girl from the Indus Valley, 2300–1750 BCE

3200 BCE

Ornate metal objects like this statue were made in Egypt and the Indus Valley. An artist first carved the object in wood and used it to make an impression in wet clay. Molten copper or bronze poured into the dip hardened in the right shape.

3100 BCE

The **Babylonian number system** emerged, based around the number 60 rather than 10. This still survives in our use of 60 minutes in an hour and 360 degrees in a circle, fixed by Babylonian astronomers and never changed. Just as we count to ten and then start a new column, so we have 1s, 10s, 100s, and so on, Babylonians counted to 60 and then had a new column. So their numbers were arranged as 1s, 60s, 3,600s, and so on. Within that, they had two symbols: one for units (ones) and one for tens.

3200 BCE

Iron from meteors was hammered into shape to make **beads** and other objects.

3000 BCE

Using a shadoof to lift a heavy bucket of river water

3000 BCE

The **"shadoof"** was used in Mesopotamia to lift water in a bucket from a river, pool, or well. A heavy counterweight lifted the filled bucket. With a shadoof, people could water their crops more easily, since the work of lifting was done by the lever, not the farmworker.

CHAPTER 2

FIRST THOUGHTS

With the invention of writing, people could record and pass on scientific ideas as well as other information. Among the earliest scientific accounts are medical and astronomical texts. Astronomical records relate to the stars, planets, and events such as eclipses and comets. Medical records tell us which ailments and injuries early physicians could try and treat and some of the medicines they used.

The most important innovation of the period 3000 BCE to 499 CE came right toward the end of the period. That was the whole idea of science—of finding rational explanations for natural phenomena and things that happen in the world. The notion that the world can be explained and that one thing reliably causes another, underpins all of science and still lies at the heart of what scientists do.

During the later part of this period, we sometimes know precise dates of events and ideas, but where the date is known only roughly, it's shown as "c." standing for *circa* (around).

WRITING

The historic era began with the invention of writing. Using written words and numbers meant that people could record information, including scientific ideas, and share it over time and distance.

NUMBERS

Recording numbers began before writing. People have used **tally sticks**—in which a mark stands for an object (such as a sheep) or an interval of time (such as a day)—since prehistoric times. You don't need symbols to represent numbers—or even the ability to count—to use a tally stick.

Counting and recording numbers in the abstract, rather than a tally or count, began around 6000 BCE in Syria and Iran. People began to record possessions by putting a clay cone for each object (perhaps a chicken or a sheep) in a container and marking the contents on the outside—four chicken symbols to show that the person owned four chickens, for example. Soon, they stopped using the tokens inside. The Egyptians started to use different symbols for different quantities rather than repeating the object-symbol. This meant that they could build up much larger numbers.

Tally stick

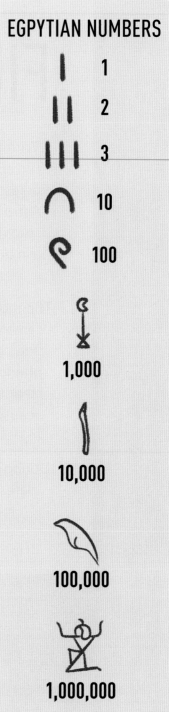

EGPYTIAN NUMBERS

I	1
II	2
III	3
∩	10
ℓ	100
	1,000
	10,000
	100,000
	1,000,000

HOW TO WRITE NUMBERS IN EGYPTIAN HIEROGLYPHS

This example of **hieroglyphs** shows how the number 4,622 would be written as four symbols for 1,000, six symbols for 100, and two each of the symbols for 10 and for 1.

4,622 →

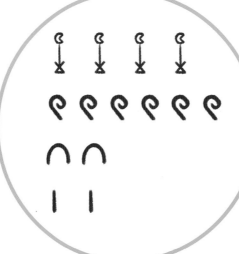

WORDS

The earliest possible examples of writing, found in Europe, Easter Island, and the Indus Valley, all date from around 5500 BCE. But as none of these has been interpreted, we can't be absolutely sure that they are writing.

The oldest certain writing is from Mesopotamia around 3400–3300 BCE. People began writing separately in other places—in Egypt (around 3250 BCE), China (1200 BCE), and Southern Mexico and Guatemala (around 900–650 BCE).

The Kish tablet from Sumer with pictograms, dating from 3500 BCE, may be the earliest known writing

The earliest writing was **pictograms**—little pictures that look like the things they stand for. The sign for barley (right) looks like a barley stalk.

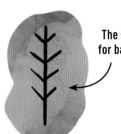

The sign for barley

In Mesopotamia, signs were pressed into a slab of soft clay with a reed. Over time, signs become more stylized. The type of tools used also affected how symbols looked.

When the Sumerians switched from a reed to a triangular, wedge-shaped stylus, their symbols lost their curves and became angular—a style called cuneiform.

Chinese and Egyptian writing also began with pictograms that gradually became more abstract over time.

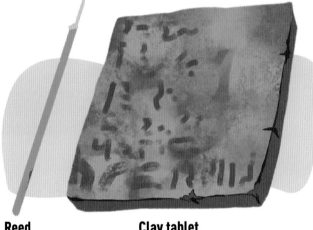

Reed   **Clay tablet**

Cuneiform writing

Wedge-shaped stylus

In languages that use pictograms or hieroglyphs, each symbol represents a word or a syllable. This type of system needs lots of symbols.

Early Egyptian hieroglyphs, probably giving the names of people or places

HOW THE WORD "FISH" CHANGED

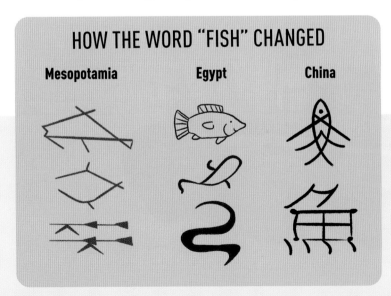

Mesopotamia   **Egypt**   **China**

Another type of writing represents the sounds of a spoken word. Western alphabets do this. Each letter stands for a sound, and several are put together to make a word. Many fewer symbols are needed, so learning to read and write is easier.

3000–2001 BCE

Five thousand years ago, civilizations grew in the Middle East and North Africa. The region around Iraq and Egypt had fertile farmland. Plentiful food meant that people had the opportunity to make advances in areas such as technology, medicine, and astronomy.

3000 BCE

Egyptian astronomers discovered that a **year** has 365 days.

2800 BCE

The first **soap,** which was used in Sumeria, was a mix of ashes and water. It was probably first used to wash the grease out of wool before making fabric.

3000 BCE

The Egyptians use **standardized units** for measuring. Recognizing a unit of length was necessary for building the pyramids, which involved many workers cooperating.

2900 BCE

The Egyptians wrote on **papyrus**, a material they made by splitting reeds. Ink and paperlike materials made writing quicker and easier than pressing designs into clay.

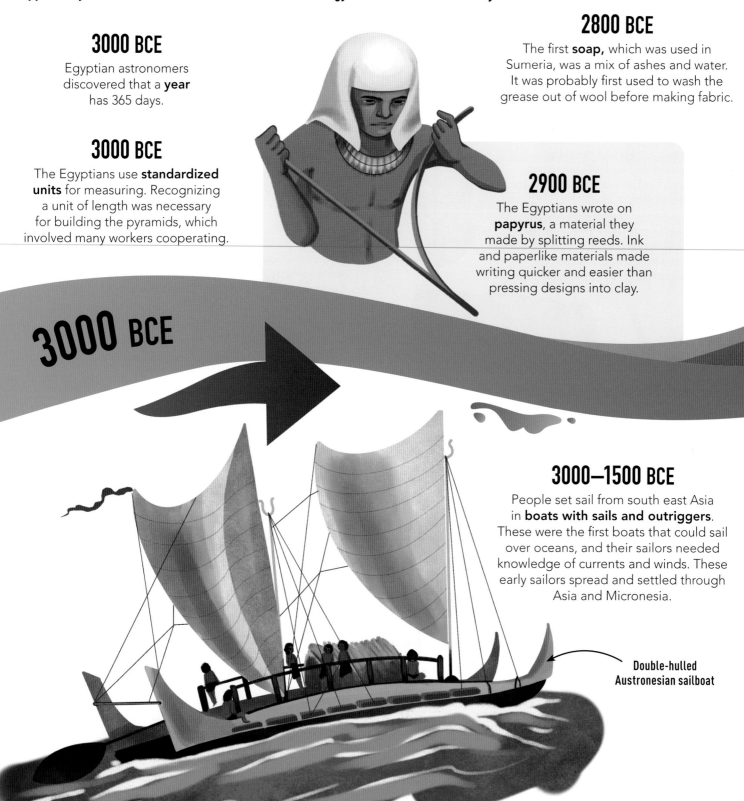

3000 BCE

3000–1500 BCE

People set sail from south east Asia in **boats with sails and outriggers**. These were the first boats that could sail over oceans, and their sailors needed knowledge of currents and winds. These early sailors spread and settled through Asia and Micronesia.

Double-hulled Austronesian sailboat

2700–1700 BCE

With improved **tools**, such as a saw with a toothed blade and a metal needle with an eye, people of the Indus Valley could make many objects more efficiently and precisely.

Metal needle

2400 BCE

Traders in Mesopotamia arranged pebbles on a board or tray of sand to make a **counting board**. By dividing the pebbles into rows, they could do calculations quickly and easily. This was an early form of abacus.

2500 BCE

People in Mexico performed **dentistry** by replacing missing back teeth with wolf teeth.

2650 BCE

A Sumerian copper bar marked with regular divisions is possibly the oldest surviving **tool for measuring length**. It's nearly 52 cm (20.5 in) long.

2001 BCE

2600 BCE

The Egyptian Imhotep is the first **medical doctor** whose name has survived. He probably wrote a text that describes many medical conditions, with treatments and likely outcomes. It explains how to stop bleeding, how to stitch wounds, how to drill into the skull, and also describes the brain. It is the earliest example of treating medicine in a scientific way. The text he probably wrote survives only in a later copy.

2500 BCE

The Sumerians used **wheeled chariots in war,** perhaps as attack vehicles or just for transporting people and weapons.

2000–1251 BCE

People in widely separated civilizations independently made similar discoveries and inventions. Although people in South America, China, and North Africa were not in touch with each other, their knowledge developed in similar directions. All studied the stars, recorded their findings, and made astronomical predictions, for example.

Knotted rope for calculating land distances and areas

1900 BCE

The Mokaya people in Mexico made a drink from the **cocoa** plant.

1800 BCE

The Rhind papyrus from Egypt reports **measuring land** using rope with evenly spaced knots. The annual flooding of the Nile meant that Egyptian land had to be remeasured to mark out fields after the flooding.

2000 BCE

1800 BCE

Metalworkers in Turkey first made **steel**—iron with some added carbon—which is stronger and harder than iron alone. Steel was probably first discovered by leaving iron in charcoal furnaces longer than usual, allowing it to absorb carbon from the charcoal.

1700 BCE

The **woolly mammoth** became extinct, with the final individuals dying out on Wrangel Island off the coast of Russia.

1700 BCE

The Sumerians grouped days into **weeks** and split the day into **24 hours**.

Pleiades

1800 BCE

The oldest detailed astronomical tool is the **Nebra sky disk**, a bronze disk 30 cm (12 in) across found in Germany. It was probably used to calculate when to add a leap month to keep the solar (Sun-based) and lunar (Moon-based) calendars in step.

A lunar month is 29 ½ days long, so there are 12 ⅓ lunar months in a year. When the Moon and the Pleiades (a group of stars shown by seven spots), were in the positions shown on the disk—roughly every three years—it was time to add a month.

Moon

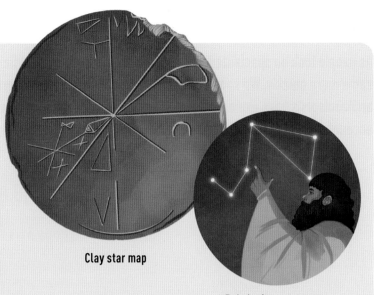

1650 BCE

Babylonian astronomers recorded their careful observations of **Venus** over 21 years.

1530–1155 BCE

The oldest **star guide** includes many ancient names for stars, suggesting that it was based on an earlier, lost version perhaps made circa 3500 BCE. Early astronomers used the movements of the stars and planets across the sky to track the calendar, and for astrology and religious purposes.

Clay star map

Babylonian astronomer

1251 BCE

1600 BCE

People in Mesopotamia began to make hollow **glass objects**, forming them around a core of sand.

1450 BCE

Sundials were used in Egypt to tell the time of day.

1600 BCE

Egyptian surgeons reconstructed noses for people who had lost them in battle or as a punishment. This was the first **plastic surgery**. The earliest record is from around 1600 BCE, but the practice may be older, perhaps even from 3000 BCE. We don't know the method used in Egypt, but in the the sixth century BCE, Indian surgeons lifted a flap of skin from the forehead and folded it down to become a nose. Straws kept the nostrils open while it healed.

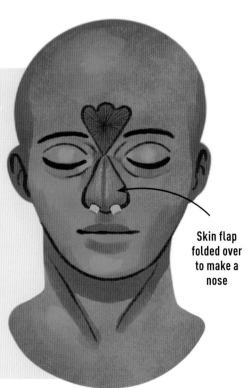

Skin flap folded over to make a nose

1250–1200 BCE

The earliest form of **Chinese characters** was a script scratched into oracle bones— pieces of bone and tortoiseshell used to divine fortunes.

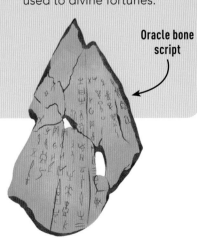

Oracle bone script

1250–501 BCE

As people took on specialized work in the growing cities, scientific advances came more quickly. We know most about progress in regions where archaeologists have explored the relics of buildings, objects, and written accounts that people left behind, including the Middle East and China.

1150 BCE

In Egypt, the oldest **geological map** shows the location of gold mines and different kinds of stone found in the region.

950–710 BCE

The oldest surviving **prosthetic (artificial) body part** is a strap-on wooden toe from Egypt. Toes are essential to our balance, so this would have been important to the patient.

Replacement toe made of wood

1000 BCE

The Babylonian **MUL.APIN tablets** (see page 42) give the dates of the first appearance in the year of important stars and lists constellations (patterns in the stars), including some that are still recognized. The star positions would have been accurate around 1000 BCE, although the surviving tablets were made later, so are copies of an earlier record.

1200 BCE

The first-known **chemist** was a Mesopotamian woman named Tapputi. She developed methods for extracting scents from flowers and wood, distilled scented oils, and developed some of the methods of making perfumes still used today. People used perfumes on their bodies, but scents were also important offerings to the gods.

850 BCE

The Indian astronomer Yajnavalkya suggested a model of the **solar system** in which Earth is spherical and goes around the Sun, along with the other planets.

800 BCE

Farmers in Egypt pollinated date palms with a brush, showing that they understood the importance of **pollination** in setting fruit.

700 BCE

Etruscans in Italy used **human or animal teeth** attached to the person's remaining teeth with gold wires.

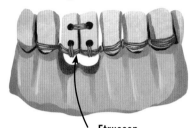

Etruscan replacement teeth were wired to remaining teeth

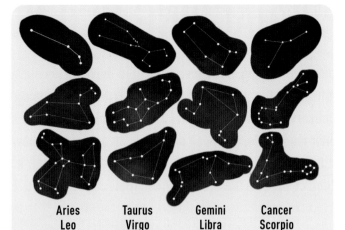

Aries	Taurus	Gemini	Cancer
Leo	Virgo	Libra	Scorpio
Sagittarius	Capricorn	Aquarius	Pisces

700–600 BCE

Babylonian astronomers identified Mercury, Venus, Mars, Jupiter, and Saturn, recorded the movements of Venus, and identified 12 **constellations of the zodiac**.

500 BCE

Natural gas was first used as a fuel in China. It was transported in bamboo pipelines from where it seeped out of the ground, to Sichuan, where it was used to boil seawater to extract salt.

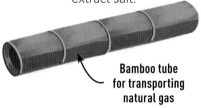

Bamboo tube for transporting natural gas

501 BCE

Sushruta

600–501 BCE

Removing a cataract from a patient's eye

The Indian **physician** Sushruta lived in northern India. His true name is not known; Sushruta means "famous." He is considered the father of surgery. His book on medicine gives instructions for surgery, including rebuilding noses, treating cataracts (a cloudy lens in the eye), amputations, dealing with childbirth, and removing metal splinters with a magnet. Cataract surgery was mentioned in Babylon around 1750 BCE, but not described.

Sushruta recommended exercise and healthy diet to avoid illness, listed 300 human bones, and identified the brain as the seat of understanding. His students learned to stitch wounds using vegetables and examined corpses to learn about the human body. He hung bodies in a basket in a river to decompose, in order to reveal the layers and finally bones without breaking laws against cutting dead bodies.

Trainee surgeon sewing up a "wound" on a squash

600–501 BCE

Steel with a high carbon content, known as **Wootz steel**, was the best steel made anywhere in the world and was exported from Sri Lanka (where it was made) to China, the Arab world, and Europe. It was easily identified by its natural swirly patterns.

APPROACHING SCIENCE

Before the development of writing, our ancestors could leave no account of how they saw the world, nor any scientific ideas that they might have had. With the beginning of writing, we can see evidence of careful observation in the star guides that people left and an attempt to understand the human body in their medical texts. These don't give an overview of how people thought about scientific topics, though. The first glimpse of something we might call a scientific mind and scientific method came with the Greek thinker Thales of Miletus (c. 620–c. 546 BCE).

THE FIRST SCIENTIST

Thales was the first person we know of who set out to explain the world in terms of physical causes and effects. For this reason, he is sometimes called the "first scientist." Thales used practical methods to investigate phenomena that he wanted to explain, and he tried to draw out general principles or rules from his discoveries. He valued knowledge for its own sake, and believed that the workings of the universe could be discovered through careful investigation and thought. He rejected the idea of mysteries that can't be explained or events caused by gods.

Thales of Miletus was a mathematician, astronomer, and philosopher. He set Ancient Greece on the path toward science as we now think of it

A WET WORLD

Thales believed that all matter came from water. It might sound strange to us, but it fitted his observations of the world. He could see water change between solid (ice), liquid, and gas as it heated and cooled.

He would have seen sediment (soil and sand) building up near Miletus, deposited from the river Maeander, which must have looked like soil forming from water. He thought that all things came from water by entirely natural processes. He believed, too, that Earth floated on a great ocean and that earthquakes were the result of rough conditions in the ocean. Although his explanation is wrong, it was the first attempt at a scientific account.

SILT CREATING MORE LAND IN ANCIENT TURKEY

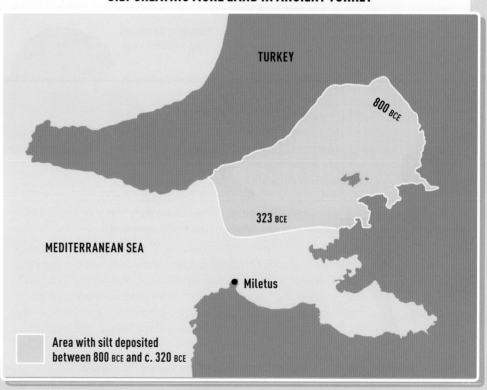

TURKEY

800 BCE

323 BCE

MEDITERRANEAN SEA

• Miletus

Area with silt deposited between 800 BCE and c. 320 BCE

SCIENCE BASED IN MATHEMATICS

Thales had learned geometry from the Egyptians and made statements that he tried to prove were correct by trying lots of different examples. This type of proof isn't considered valid now, but the idea of proving that a mathematical statement is true in all cases was a landmark in **mathematical thinking**. It shows that he considered mathematics to be universal, providing rules that apply all the time to all examples. Thales applied mathematics to his observations. He is said to have predicted a solar eclipse in 585 BCE. If he did, he calculated it from what he knew about the movements of the Sun and Moon.

SCIENCE TALK

Other Greek thinkers shared Thales' view that the universe could be explained. They debated and argued constructively about their ideas, starting a tradition of **learning through debate** that continues today. Some of their ideas have turned out to be broadly correct.

HOW ECLIPSES HAPPEN

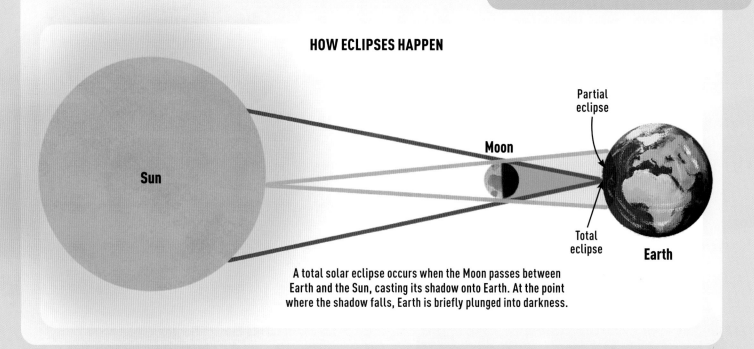

Sun

Moon

Partial eclipse

Total eclipse

Earth

A total solar eclipse occurs when the Moon passes between Earth and the Sun, casting its shadow onto Earth. At the point where the shadow falls, Earth is briefly plunged into darkness.

A CHANGING WORLD

Two thinkers who followed Thales were Anaximander and Xenophanes. Anaximander suggested that life forms first came from the mud and lived in the water. As land and sea separated, he thought some creatures adapted to live on land and that even humans had developed from these. Xenophanes correctly figured out that fossils of fish found inland were the impressions of long-dead animals, and suggested that land and sea had changed places.

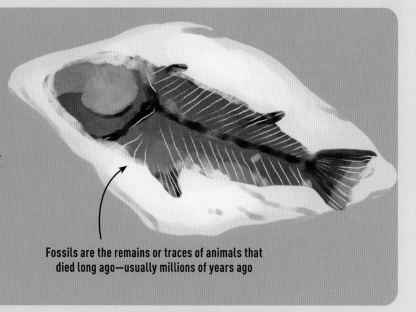

Fossils are the remains or traces of animals that died long ago—usually millions of years ago

500–301 BCE

During this period, we know most about scientific developments in Greece, where people were recording scientific thought for the first time. They were exploring ideas about the nature of the world and universe around them, not to solve practical problems but to understand how the world works.

c. 440 BCE

In Greece, Anaxagoras suggested that **Earth** had formed from matter rotating in empty space. Heavy matter was drawn inward, and light, fiery matter flew outward. Earth grew larger as it collected heavy material. He thought that the Sun and other stars formed from fiery metal and rock in a similar way.

c. 500 BCE

Indian scientist Kanada said that **matter** could be divided into very tiny pieces that could not be further split. These "parmanu" were believed to be combined in different ways, producing different types of matter. This is similar to the modern atomic theory of matter.

The Sun is a star

500 BCE

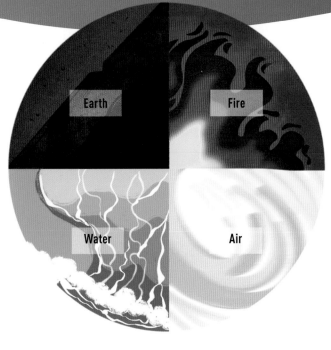

Earth

Fire

Water

Air

c. 440 BCE

Anaxagoras said that the Moon is made of rock and is lit by the Sun, rather than creating its own light. He used this model to explain **eclipses** and the **phases of the Moon**.

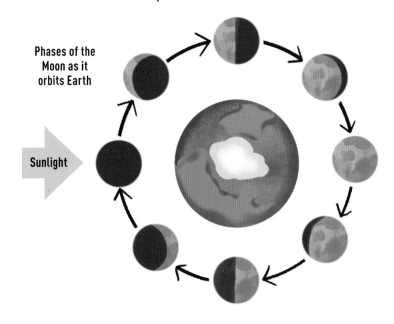

Phases of the Moon as it orbits Earth

Sunlight

c. 460 BCE

Greek thinker Empedocles declared that all matter is made of four basic "roots"—**earth, fire, water, and air**—that can be mixed and remixed to make different things. The properties of materials depend on the proportions of the roots in them.

c. 420 BCE

The Greek thinker Democritus suggested that humans once lived simply, gathering food, following the animals they hunted, and living in caves. Over many **generations**, they developed spoken language, built shelters, made clothing, developed agriculture, crafts, and written language, all in response to hardship or challenges.

c. 429 BCE

Another Greek thinker, Empedocles, claimed that the **speed of light** is finite, even though people had no way of measuring it.

c. 420 BCE

The Greek thinkers Leucippus and Democritus suggested that everything is made of an infinite number of tiny particles that can't be subdivided, which they called **"atoms"** (meaning "uncuttables"). Different kinds of atoms join to produce all the types of matter. The features of atoms give material its properties, so they thought that water atoms are smooth and can easily slide over each other, but iron is hard to break since its spiky atoms cling together. Atoms are constantly recycled, but can't be destroyed or created.

Water atoms   **Iron atoms**

301 BCE

c. 400 BCE

The Greek medical scientist Hippocrates thought that the body contains four **"humors"** or different types of fluid: blood, phlegm, black bile, and yellow bile. If these are unbalanced, a person will be sick. The cure required rebalancing their humors. People followed this advice for 2,000 years, using largely unhelpful treatments such as bloodletting to remove "unnecessary" extra blood. Hippocrates set out the job of a doctor: finding out what is wrong with a patient (diagnosis), observing their illness, and telling them what is likely to happen (prognosis).

Cast iron Chinese farming tool

400 BCE

Metalworkers in China perfected **cast iron** by mixing a small quantity of carbon into molten iron. They made plowshares (also spelled "ploughshares"), pots, weapons, and parts of pagodas. Cast iron wasn't used in the West until the fifteenth century.

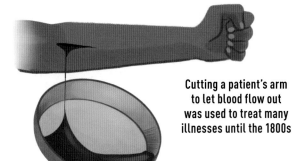

Cutting a patient's arm to let blood flow out was used to treat many illnesses until the 1800s

350–1 BCE

In Europe, the Greek and Roman civilizations were dominant. Roman engineers made great advances in technology and created buildings and roads that still survive. In China, astronomers kept records that are used even now by modern astronomers.

c. 250 BCE

Greek mathematician Archimedes explained the principle of the **lever** and the **Archimedes screw**. He also realized that an object immersed in water displaces (moves aside) its own weight of water and calculated the center of gravity of objects.

Using a lever

c. 350–301 BCE

In China, Zhuangzi suggested that animals **adapt and change** to suit their environment, and that even humans have done this. He noted that they tended to change from simple to more complex forms.

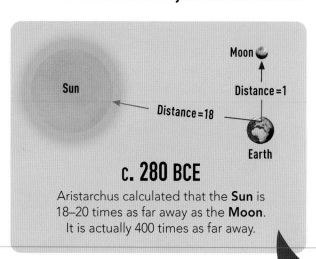

Moon

Distance = 1

Distance = 18

Sun

Earth

c. 280 BCE

Aristarchus calculated that the **Sun** is 18–20 times as far away as the **Moon**. It is actually 400 times as far away.

350 BCE

c. 350 BCE

Greek thinker Aristotle began to **classify living things** by their characteristics and features, rather than their uses to humans. Theophrastus did the same for plants soon after. He also noticed that fallen leaves enrich the soil and in doing so nourish other plants.

Aristarchus's model of the solar system, with the Sun in the middle

Saturn

Jupiter

Mars

Moon

Earth

Sun

Venus

Mercury

FROM 300 BCE

In a major feat of engineering, the Romans built about 80,000 km (50,000 miles) of **stone roads** to link the various parts of their empire. These roads had a curved surface, so that water drained to the sides, and they had ditches, bridleways, and footpaths alongside.

c. 260 BCE

Ancient Greek astronomer Aristarchus suggested that the **planets all orbit the Sun** and put them in order: Mercury (closest to the Sun), Venus, Earth, Mars, Jupiter, and Saturn. He recognized that Earth takes a year to orbit the Sun and a day to turn on its axis, and that stars seem to move around the sky only because Earth is rotating.

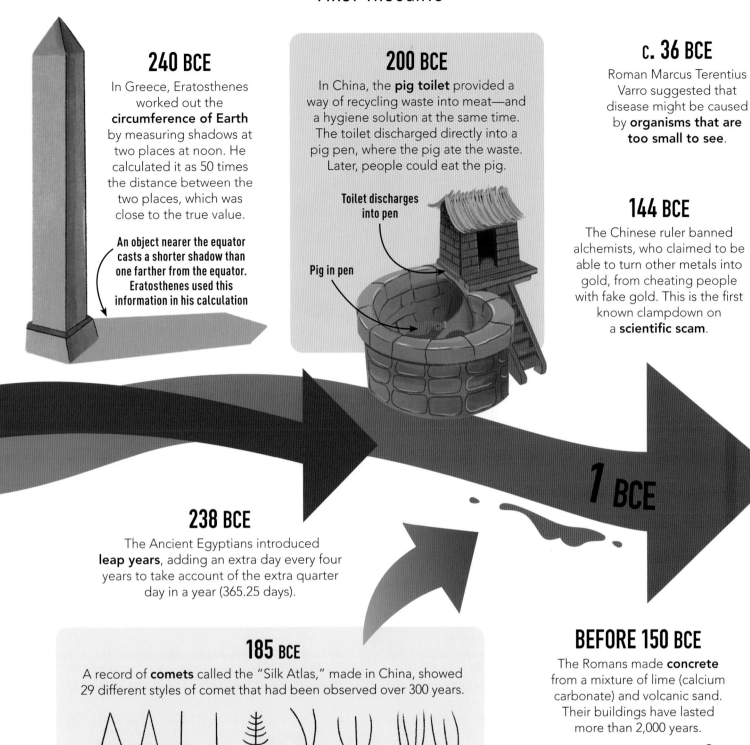

240 BCE

In Greece, Eratosthenes worked out the **circumference of Earth** by measuring shadows at two places at noon. He calculated it as 50 times the distance between the two places, which was close to the true value.

An object nearer the equator casts a shorter shadow than one farther from the equator. Eratosthenes used this information in his calculation

200 BCE

In China, the **pig toilet** provided a way of recycling waste into meat—and a hygiene solution at the same time. The toilet discharged directly into a pig pen, where the pig ate the waste. Later, people could eat the pig.

Toilet discharges into pen

Pig in pen

c. 36 BCE

Roman Marcus Terentius Varro suggested that disease might be caused by **organisms that are too small to see**.

144 BCE

The Chinese ruler banned alchemists, who claimed to be able to turn other metals into gold, from cheating people with fake gold. This is the first known clampdown on a **scientific scam**.

1 BCE

238 BCE

The Ancient Egyptians introduced **leap years**, adding an extra day every four years to take account of the extra quarter day in a year (365.25 days).

185 BCE

A record of **comets** called the "Silk Atlas," made in China, showed 29 different styles of comet that had been observed over 300 years.

Chinese pictures of comets

BEFORE 150 BCE

The Romans made **concrete** from a mixture of lime (calcium carbonate) and volcanic sand. Their buildings have lasted more than 2,000 years.

Roman Pantheon

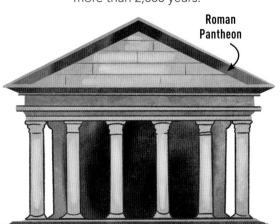

1–499 CE

During the first centuries of the Common Era (CE), China was the scene of the most significant scientific discoveries and advances. Note that we date years from 1, not 0—there is no year zero between 1 BCE and 1 CE.

1st CENTURY CE

Roman thinker Seneca produced a **spectrum** by splitting white light through a glass prism.

c. 70

Greek medical doctor Dioscorides collected all that was known about **medicines** (pharmacology) into one volume, which was used for 1,500 years.

105

In China, Cai Lun refined and popularized the manufacture of **paper**, which had begun in the 3rd century BCE.

Alembic for alchemy

1st CENTURY CE

In Egypt, according to legend, Mary the Jewess made the first **alembic**, an apparatus used in alchemy to distill liquids. A liquid is evaporated, then condensed on a lid or cover to run down a spout and be collected.

1 CE

1st CENTURY CE

Hero of Alexander, living in Greek Egypt, made the first **steam turbine** called an "aeolipile." Hot water produced steam in two jets to drive a free-spinning wheel around. It wasn't put to any practical use.

132

Chinese scientist Zhang Heng made the first **seismoscope**, a device for detecting earthquakes. Although it couldn't predict earthquakes, the vibrations of a distant earthquake would make one of the balls fall from the mouth of a dragon into that of a waiting brass frog on the side where the earthquake took place.

A ball falls from dragon's mouth into the frog's mouth below

2ⁿᵈ CENTURY CE

The Roman–Egyptian astronomer Ptolemy set out all known **astronomy** and **mapped the world** as it was known in the Roman Empire. His work was taken as accurate for centuries.

2ⁿᵈ CENTURY CE

Lucian of Samosata, in Syria, wrote a science-fiction story about **space travel**, that was intended as a satire of the fantastical travelogues written at the time.

220–280

In China, Lui Hui developed the **surveying technique** used to calculate distances such as the height of a tower or mountain, or the depth of a ravine or clear river.

Calculating the height of a mountain

c. 150–200

Chinese doctor Hua Tuo is said to have used a **general anaesthetic** for surgical operations, but no details of it have survived.

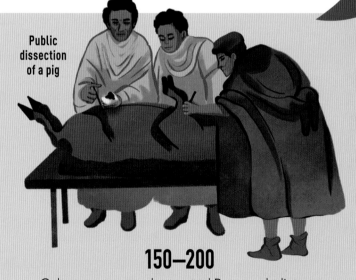

Public dissection of a pig

150–200

Galen, a surgeon who treated Roman gladiators, **dissected** (cut up) animals and wrote about the human body, assuming that human and animal bodies were the same. His textbook was used for a thousand years, even though much of it was wrong.

499 CE

480

Chinese mathematician Zu Chongzhi gave an estimate for **pi** (the ratio of a circle's circumference to its diameter) of 355/113. This remained the best estimate for 1,200 years.

499

In India, Aryabhata recognized the elliptical orbit of planets (not discovered in Europe until after 1600) and proposed that Earth turns on its axis, causing the apparent movement of stars around the sky. He correctly explained eclipses as caused by shadows falling on or cast by Earth and said that the Moon and planets shine with reflected sunlight.

ASTRONOMY

Even our very earliest ancestors looked up at the night sky and began to track the Moon, stars, and planets. They built huge structures, such as Stonehenge in England and the temples and pyramids of South America and Egypt, which lined up with sunrise at the solstice (the shortest or longest day of the year) or with the patterns of the stars. The science of astronomy enabled people to track time for farming, religious festivals, and probably personal events, such as following a pregnancy.

STARS AND PLANETS

With written records, astronomers in the Middle East and China began making **star charts** and recorded when different stars rose above the horizon to become visible for the first time in a year. Ancient astronomers saw how the planets differed from stars: They move slowly across the sky, and they don't twinkle. Planets appear to go backward sometimes in their movement across the sky. This is an effect of Earth's own movement, but no one knew that yet.

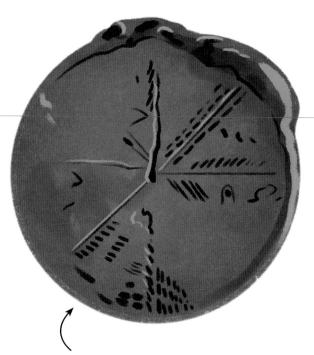

The earliest star charts are the Babylonian "three stars each" star catalogs, which were made of clay tablets before 1100 BCE. They show the positions of 36 stars

The MUL.APIN star chart on two clay tablets was made around 1000 BCE. It adds more stars and corrects information from the earlier chart

Ancient Greek astronomers built on the work of those in Mesopotamia and Egypt. They had two competing descriptions of the solar system. The **geocentric model** put Earth in the middle, with the other planets and the Sun going around it. The **heliocentric model** put the Sun in the middle, with all the planets, including Earth, orbiting it. Looking up at the sky, it is impossible to tell which model is correct—they would both look the same.

SETTING A PATTERN

One of the most important figures in the history of Western astronomy was **Ptolemy**, who lived in Egypt in the second century CE when it was part of the Roman Empire. He produced an astronomy text called *Almagest*, which was used in the West for nearly 1,500 years. It included a catalog of stars based on that of Hipparchus, a list of 48 constellations, and tables for calculating astronomical events such as the positions of the Sun, Moon, and planets, and eclipses.

Ptolemy

THE GEOCENTRIC MODEL

In Ptolemy's geocentric solar system, the Sun, Moon, and each planet sat in its own sphere around Earth. The stars were all on an outer sphere. Each sphere revolved at a different speed. He described a series of adjustments needed to make the observed movement of the planets fit his model. Ptolemy's belief that everything goes around Earth was followed by astronomers for more than 1,300 years. Although wrong, his model could be used to predict the movement of planets.

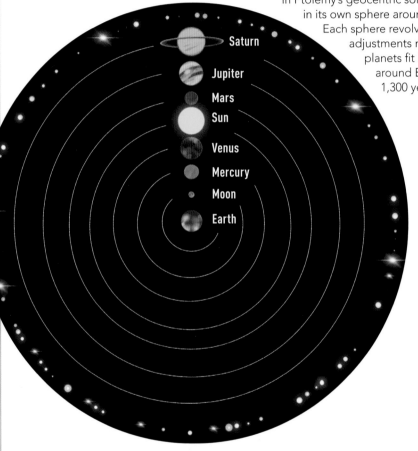

Saturn

Jupiter

Mars

Sun

Venus

Mercury

Moon

Earth

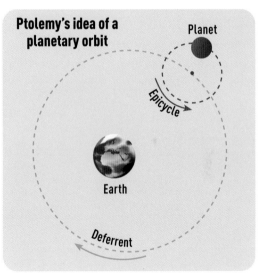

Ptolemy's idea of a planetary orbit

Planet

Epicycle

Earth

Deferrent

According to Ptolemy, each planet went around in a small circle (an epicycle), and this orbital circle went around Earth in a larger circle (a deferrent). Earth is not central in the deferrent

THE HELIOCENTRIC MODEL

In India around 500 CE, Aryabhata calculated the timing of eclipses and realized that the planets were on elliptical orbits around the Sun. He saw that the strange paths of the planets were produced by a combination of their own movement and that of Earth. Western astronomers didn't realize this for another thousand years.

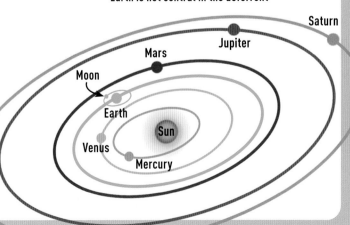

Saturn

Jupiter

Mars

Moon

Earth

Sun

Venus

Mercury

CHAPTER 3

———

EXPLORING THE WORLD

The focus of scientific activity shifted around the world a great deal in the 1,200 years from 500 CE. In the West, it moved from Greece and Egypt to the Middle East, with Baghdad at the middle of developments, until eventually it shifted back to Europe. Scientists in India and China made independent progress. As travel along the Silk Routes between China and India brought people of the East and West together, scientific ideas were shared. By 1700, European science could claim major discoveries, including the microscope and telescope, which revolutionized the way we see the world. It also saw developments in the scientific way of thinking and an eagerness to explore topics without direct practical applications, such as the age of Earth or the structure of the solar system. This was a big step forward from the largely practical nature of science in previous centuries.

500–999 CE

For five centuries, the focus of scientific progress was in the East. In China and in the countries of the Arab world, scientists built on the work of their predecessors, experimenting, thinking, and then recording their findings.

SIXTH CENTURY

Thinkers of the Vaisheshika school in India thought of **light** as a fast-moving stream of "fire atoms." This is similar to the modern concept of photons as tiny particles of light energy.

577

An early type of **match** was made in China by impregnating small sticks of pinewood with sulfur (also spelled sulphur) They caught light at the slightest touch of fire.

c. 525

In Egypt, John Philoponus realized that the **weight** of a falling object doesn't affect the **speed** at which it falls.

593

Woodblock printing was first mentioned in China. Each page to be printed had to be carved in wood. It was then covered with ink, and paper was pressed against the woodblock to make an impression.

754

The first **apothecary shops** opened in Baghdad (now Iraq). These were the earliest form of pharmacies.

500 CE

532–537

Isidore of Miletus designed a new church of **Hagia Sophia** in Constantinople (now Istanbul), in Turkey, to replace one that had been destroyed in riots. He planned it without using wood, so that it couldn't burn. It was a great feat of mechanical engineering that used vaulting designed to hold up the dome without obvious structural supports.

NINTH CENTURY

In his *Book of Animals*, al-Jahiz (776–868) in Iraq classified creatures in a sequence from what he considered the simplest to the most complex and divided them into groups based on their similarities. It was an early attempt to **categorize animals** just as themselves, without referring to how humans used them. He also suggested food webs, showing how organisms depend on each other for food.

NINTH CENTURY

In Syria, astronomers calculated the **circumference of Earth**, gaining a figure close to that accepted today.

919

The **flamethrower** was developed in China as a military weapon using liquid fuel.

Pulling and pushing the handle on the left of the tube pumps flammable liquid from the tank below into the flamethrower

832

The **House of Wisdom** was founded in Baghdad as a place of scholarship where experts translated and commented on the works of the Ancient Greeks and others. Arab scientists often built on the texts to explore science further. The Arab versions were later translated into Latin, bringing them to Europe.

999 CE

c. 980

In Iran, al-Majusi pointed out the close relationship between physical and mental health, and described **psychosomatic illness**. This is when a mental state causes physical symptoms (such as getting a stomachache when nervous).

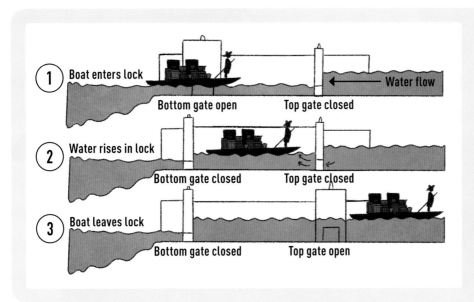

① Boat enters lock — Water flow
Bottom gate open — Top gate closed

② Water rises in lock
Bottom gate closed — Top gate closed

③ Boat leaves lock
Bottom gate closed — Top gate open

984

Chiao Wei-yo developed a type of lock, now called the **pound lock**, to use on the canals of China. A boat enters a pool of water separated by two gates from the upper and lower parts of a canal. The water level is raised or lowered in the pool, and the boat is then released into the next portion of the canal.

1000–1249

Arab scientists spent a lot of time studying light and lenses, laying the groundwork for much of the later work on light. They were also excellent medical scientists and made great progress in making and using surgical instruments and treating illness.

Ibn Sina
980–1037

Ibn Sina was a **medical doctor** born in Uzbekistan. His books were widely used in North Africa and Europe until 1650. He described many diseases, injuries, and treatments, outlined the structure of the eye, and explained how to treat cataracts (cloudy lenses in the eye). Ibn Sina argued that it's impossible to turn cheap metals into gold, which was a main aim of alchemy. He suggested that fossils are made when the bodies of animals are drenched with a "petrifying fluid" that turns them to stone.

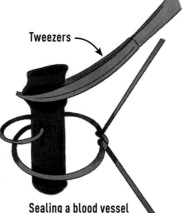

c. 1000

The Spanish-Arab surgeon al-Zahrawi invented **surgical instruments**, including the surgical needle and forceps. He began using catgut for stitches inside the body, and he tied off blood vessels to stem the blood flow in injuries.

Tweezers

Sealing a blood vessel with a stitch

1000

1010–1021

Arab scientist al-Haytham explained **how we see**: Light reflected from objects travels to the eye, and the brain makes an image from it. Previously, people thought that beams of light came from the eye to seize an image. Al-Haytham used a camera obscura to explain light entering the eye and making an image.

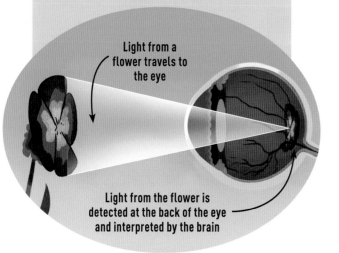

Light from a flower travels to the eye

Light from the flower is detected at the back of the eye and interpreted by the brain

c. 1010

The English monk Eilmer of Malmesbury strapped on large kite-like wings and launched himself into the air from a tower, becoming the first person to succeed in making a **flight**. He flew 200 m (656 ft), but he broke both legs when he landed and was lame thereafter.

1037

In Uzbekistan, al-Biruni predicted there must be a **large landmass** to the west of the Atlantic (where the Americas are) and that it would be inhabited. He based this on his calculation that Eurasia occupies only two-fifths of Earth, so there should be more land.

c. 1080

The Chinese scientist Shen Kuo described **climate change** and changes in the landscape after noticing bamboo fossils where bamboo no longer grew, the buildup of silt, and other changes. He discovered that geological features are made by wind and rain wearing away rocks. Some of his ideas sound very modern. He thought of using insects that eat pests to protect crops and worried that the iron-smelting industry and the use of pine soot to make ink would lead to deforestation.

MID-THIRTEENTH CENTURY

In Syria, ibn al-Nafis described the **circulation of the blood**, showing that the beating heart sends blood around the body. He realized that blood doesn't pass directly between the two sides of the heart, but goes to the lungs from the heart, then returns to the other side of the heart.

c. 1050

In China, Sun Sikong explained that **rainbows** are produced by sunlight interacting with rain.

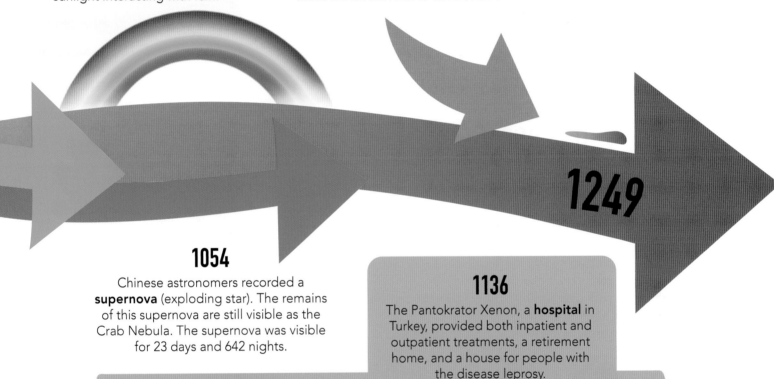

1249

1054

Chinese astronomers recorded a **supernova** (exploding star). The remains of this supernova are still visible as the Crab Nebula. The supernova was visible for 23 days and 642 nights.

1136

The Pantokrator Xenon, a **hospital** in Turkey, provided both inpatient and outpatient treatments, a retirement home, and a house for people with the disease leprosy.

FROM FIREWORKS TO FIREARMS: GUNPOWDER

The earliest chemists were alchemists who tried to find a potion to produce eternal life or looked for a way to turn ordinary metals into gold. Alchemy emerged independently in China and the Middle East about 2,000 years ago. Chinese alchemists made a black powder around 850 CE, which they called "fire medicine." It was made from sulfur, saltpeter (potassium nitrate), and charcoal (burnt wood). It didn't bring eternal life, but turned out to be one of the most deadly inventions in Earth's history—gunpowder.

Fireworks

IT IS ROCKET SCIENCE

The mixture was highly inflammable: If a flame touched it, it would explode. The alchemists quickly put gunpowder to work making **fireworks**. They found that if they burned a bamboo tube packed with gunpowder, gas whooshed from the back of it, pushing the tube forward at great speed. This is how rockets work: burning fuel quickly in a small space and using the gas produced to blast the rocket forward. When the pressure inside the bamboo tube became too great, it exploded spectacularly. Fireworks became popular, since the noise and light were thought to scare away demons.

Pottery container filled with gunpowder as an early hand grenade or bomb

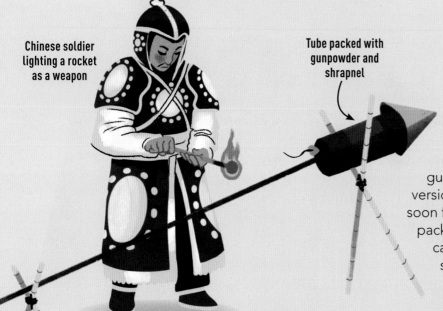

Chinese soldier lighting a rocket as a weapon

Tube packed with gunpowder and shrapnel

DEADLY POWDER

Demons were not the only victims of gunpowder. Fireworks soon became **weapons**. By 904 CE, Chinese warriors began firing flaming arrows attached to a tube of gunpowder at their enemies, the Mongols. Early versions of bombs, hand grenades, and landmines soon followed. The first attempt at a gun had a tube packed with gunpowder and sharp pieces of metal called shrapnel. Lighting the powder hurled the shrapnel at the enemy, causing terrible injuries. By the late 1200s, the Chinese had metal guns that were even more deadly.

OUT OF CHINA

The Chinese were worried about other countries acquiring **gunpowder**, and in 1076 banned the sale of saltpeter to foreigners. Even so, the secret got out. The Mongols took gunpowder to India in 1221, then to Persia and Egypt by 1260. Recipes for gunpowder were available in Europe from 1267. The first **guns** in the Middle East appeared by 1304, when the Arabs produced a bamboo tube reinforced with iron that used "black powder" to shoot an arrow.

THE SPREAD OF GUNPOWDER WITH THE MONGOL EMPIRE

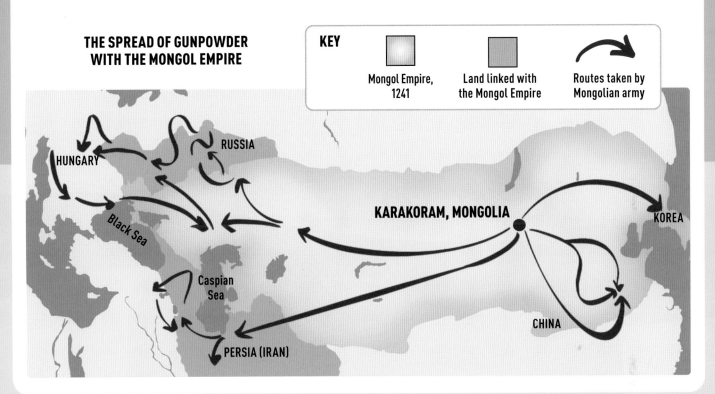

KEY

Mongol Empire, 1241

Land linked with the Mongol Empire

Routes taken by Mongolian army

RUSSIA

HUNGARY

Black Sea

KARAKORAM, MONGOLIA

KOREA

Caspian Sea

CHINA

PERSIA (IRAN)

GUNPOWDER SHAPES THE WORLD

The impact of gunpowder was immense. It was widely used to make **cannons**, which fired a heavy metal ball or many smaller balls, injuring armies or blasting through walls. Cannons could also be installed on ships, completely changing battles at sea. **Guns** gave a great advantage to any attacker who had them. Europeans invaded and easily conquered South America, North America, and sub-Saharan Africa because they had guns and the indigenous people defending their lands did not.

The fourteenth--century "divine flying fire crow" was a rocket-propelled bomb that flew through the air

1250–1499

In the late medieval period, many more scientific advances took place in Europe. The development of printing meant that scientific ideas could be easily shared, and people could build on each other's work.

Roger Bacon
1219/20–1292

The English thinker Roger Bacon promoted writing about and teaching science, and he even suggested teaching sciences in **universities**. He aimed to record all the science known in his time and extend that knowledge. He wrote about optics (how light behaves), including how to use a lens to start a fire, how to use lenses to correct vision, and even how to make a telescope, but he probably didn't make one.

1269

In France, Pierre Pelerin de Maricourt wrote the first book about the properties of **magnets**.

c. 1288

The first **glasses**, made in Italy, were hinged, perched on the nose, and had no "arms." They had convex lenses and were used for reading.

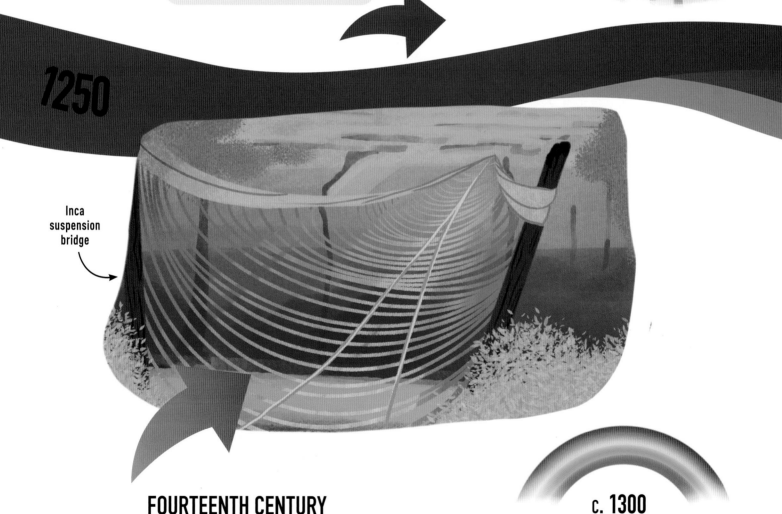

1250

Inca suspension bridge

FOURTEENTH CENTURY

Inca engineers came up with a clever solution for crossing the mountain gorges of Peru: **suspension bridges**. They made them from ichu grass woven in large bundles, which was light and very strong. They replaced the suspending ropes every year.

c. 1300

In Germany, Theoderic of Freiburg explained how a **rainbow** is formed by sunlight being refracted through raindrops.

1315

At the university of Bologna in Italy, **dissection** was used to show medical students the structures of the human body and for autopsies to investigate the cause of death.

1330

Hu Sihui, in Mongol China, stressed the importance of a **good diet** for staying healthy.

c. 1437

Persian astronomer Ulugh Beg made a **catalog of 992 stars**, which finally replaced that made by Ptolemy 1,300 years before. He calculated the length of a year to within 25 seconds.

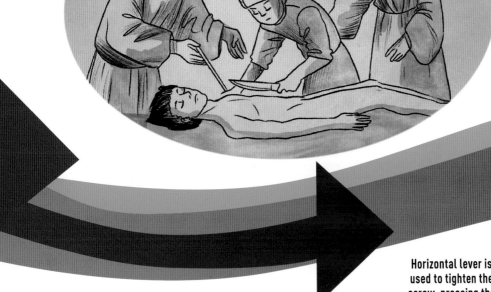

1499

Horizontal lever is used to tighten the screw, pressing the paper against the print

Paper is pressed against movable metal type

A deadly plague now known as the Black Death started in the Far East in 1346 and spread through Asia, Europe, and parts of Africa until 1351. It killed up to half the population where it struck. Many people believed it was sent as a punishment because they had angered their gods. They tried spiritual remedies, such as praying, building places of worship, or whipping themselves. Most medical "cures" would have done no good, and some did extra harm, since no one knew about germs.

Preparing coffins for plague victims

1440

In Germany, Johannes Gutenberg used a **printing press** with movable metal type. This meant that many copies of a book could be produced in a short time, while previously each had to be copied by hand. It revolutionized the spread of information, including scientific information. As books became easily available, more and more people learned to read.

1500–1549

The 1500s were the start of a period of revolutionary scientific change and discovery concentrated in western Europe. Countries in central Europe, and in particular Italy and Germany, were at the forefront of scientific developments.

1510

The first known **flu pandemic** started in Asia and spread to Europe and parts of Africa. It possibly killed one in every 100 people infected. Earlier localized epidemics of flu had probably happened since the ninth century.

1501

Amerigo Vespucci claimed that **South America** was a new continent, not part of Asia. Originally, people had set off to sail west from Europe, expecting to go around the world and end up in Asia—they had no knowledge of the Americas.

The first European map to include the Americas showed just a long strip of the coastline

1510

German clockmaker Peter Henlein made the first modern mechanical **clock** and the first portable **watch**, called the Nuremberg egg.

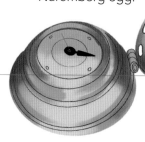

Nuremberg egg

1500

Leonardo da Vinci
1452–1519

Italian **scientist, artist, and inventor** Leonardo da Vinci is widely considered one of the greatest geniuses who ever lived. As well as making stunning works of art, including the world-famous *Mona Lisa*, he studied anatomy and drew detailed diagrams of the human body and many types of animals. His intersts were wide and varied. He also studied plants, geology, optics, and civil engineering. His drawings included many inventions that could not be made at the time, including a helicopter, a parachute, and a tank. He worked on several engineering projects, including one to redirect the Arno River in Italy. He was the first person to state the laws of friction that slow down objects moving against each other, and he said that perpetual motion is impossible to achieve: Nothing set in motion on Earth will continue moving forever. He wrote his work in code in notebooks and didn't publish his ideas, so he had little impact on developments in science.

1530s

Swiss physician Paracelsus suggested that digestion is carried out by "hungry acid" in the stomach and so is a chemical process. He was the first person known to view the body as a **chemical system**.

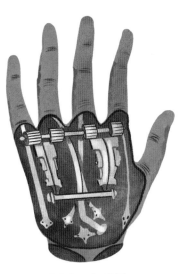

1536–1537

French surgeon Ambroise Paré tried new ways of treating wounds on the battlefield. Instead of burning the ends of cut blood vessels in wounds and amputations, he tied off blood vessels and applied oil, honey, and egg yolk to help soothe and heal them. In 1550, he even made a moving **mechanical hand** for a person who had lost their hand.

1539

Italian surgeon Andreas Vesalius challenged the ideas of Galen, which were still taught in medical schools, showing him to have been wrong about many things. Vesalius published a book in 1543 with illustrations of the bones, muscles, and other parts of the body. It revolutionized the study of **anatomy**.

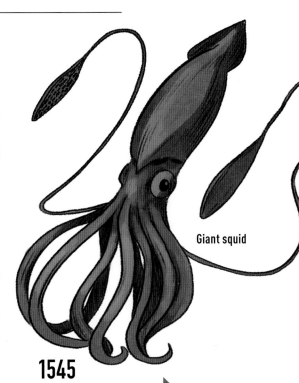

Giant squid

1545

Sailors first began to report the existence of **giant squids**, said to grow up to 13 m (42 ½ ft) long.

1549

1531

In Germany, Peter Apian noted that the **tail of a comet** always points away from the Sun.

Comet's tail

1543

Polish astronomer Nicolaus Copernicus suggested that the planets, including Earth, all **orbit the Sun** (see page 59). Although this was right, it was not accepted by many people at the time, and later the Catholic Church made it a crime to teach this idea.

1546

In Italy, Girolamo Fracastoro suggestedthat **epidemics of disease** might be caused by very tiny "spores" or "seeds" that can travel between people with or without contact. It's not clear if he thought they were living (such as microbes) or only chemical.

1545

Ambroise Paré described new ways of treating wounds. He advised against burning the ends of cut blood vessels in wounds and amputations, but tying off blood vessels instead, and applying oil, honey, and egg yolk.

1550–1599

Confidence in science was growing, and the the world was opening up in new ways in the 1500s. Travel to the Americas and elsewhere revealed animals never seen before and presented new challenges to mapmaking. The most important development was the invention of the microscope at the end of the century, changing forever how we see the world around us.

1557

French surgeon Ambroise Paré noticed that maggots eat dead and infected flesh, **cleaning a wound** so that it can heal.

1569

The Belgian mapmaker Gerardus Mercator used the **Mercator map projection** to show the spherical world on a flat piece of paper. Some countries are distorted to fit, with areas near the poles shown larger than they really are and regions near the equator shown smaller.

A modern map using the Mercator projection. Mercator's own maps did not show Australia and New Zealand (which were unknown) or accurate shapes for the Americas and Greenland

1550

1551–1558

In Switzerland, Conrad Gessner wrote the first **zoology book**, a textbook of all known animals based on observation, dissection, and accurate descriptions. He tried to be scientifically rigorous but included some creatures, such as mermaids and unicorns, that we now know don't exist. He also wrote the first book on fossils and invented the graphite pencil.

Unicorn

Gessner's illustrations of animals were not drawn from life and were inaccurate in some details

Ostrich

Tiger

Beaver

1572

A **supernova** was seen around the world and recorded by astronomers.

1582

The modern **Gregorian calendar** was introduced in some parts of Europe to correct errors in the Julian calendar introduced by the Romans 1,500 years earlier. It refined the use of leap years to keep the calendar in line with the movement of Earth around the Sun.

1584

Italian thinker Giordano Bruno wrote of an **infinite universe** that contains other worlds, one of many things he said that annoyed the Church. He was burned at the stake for his views in 1600.

1598

Sailors from the West saw **dodos** for the first time in Mauritius. Dodos would be extinct within 100 years, killed by hunting and by rats brought to the island, which ate their eggs and young.

1599

1576

In his **astronomy book**, the English astronomer Leonard Digges showed the stars scattered through infinite space, rather than all being the same distance from Earth.

c. 1595

The first **compound micrcoscope** (one with more than one lens) was invented in Holland, giving magnfication up to about 9x. It replaced the simple magnifying glasses or "flea glasses" often used for looking at tiny insects. With microscopes, people went on to discover microorganisms and the invisibly small structures of human and other bodies.

1577

Danish astronomer Tycho Brahe showed that **comets** are not within Earth's atmosphere, but are out in space (see page 58).

1593

The **thermoscope** was invented in Italy, the first step toward the thermometer. In warm conditions, the air in the bulb at the top of a glass tube expanded, pushing liquid down the tube. In colder conditions, the air contracted and more liquid went up the tube. Now, thermometers have a scale and are the other way up, with the bulb at the bottom and a taller column of liquid showing a higher temperature.

Air

Liquid

THE UNIVERSE REIMAGINED

Until 1543, everyone in Europe followed Ptolemy in believing that the Sun and other planets go around Earth. In that year, the dying astronomer Nicolaus Copernicus published a book in which he suggested a new model: The Sun is in the middle of the solar system, and all the planets orbit around it. His book did not persuade many people at first, but the world was about to see a revolution in astronomy.

BRILLIANT SKIES

The second half of the sixteenth century saw two great astronomical events. The first was a **supernova**—the explosion of a dying, distant star—which lit up the sky even in daytime, appearing like a new star. At the time, astronomers did not believe the stars could ever change, so this was hard to explain. The Danish astronomer Tycho Brahe showed that the star really was far away and not just something in Earth's atmosphere.

Brahe's comet of 1577 as it was recorded at the time when people believed that comets flew below the clouds

Tycho Brahe was the last important astronomer in the West to work without a telescope. He was also famous for having a fake metal nose and a pet moose

A few years later, in 1577, a bright **comet** appeared. This was also shown to be distant. Previously, people had thought comets were closer to Earth's surface than to the Moon. These two events were serious challenges to how people in Europe thought about the universe, which the Church taught had been set up by God to be unchanging.

NO LONGER CENTRAL

In 1609, the German astronomer Johannes Kepler showed that Earth and the other planets follow **elliptical**, not circular, paths around the Sun. This removed the need for the complicated epicycles needed to the make the Ptolemaic solar system match how the planets seemed to move. Kepler corrected the problems with Copernicus's description of the heliocentric system, and his explanation became popular with astronomers. But many people found the thought distressing: It was hard to hold onto the idea of humankind's place as central to the universe if Earth was just one of several planets orbiting the Sun. It directly contradicted the Bible, causing many people to find it hard to accept.

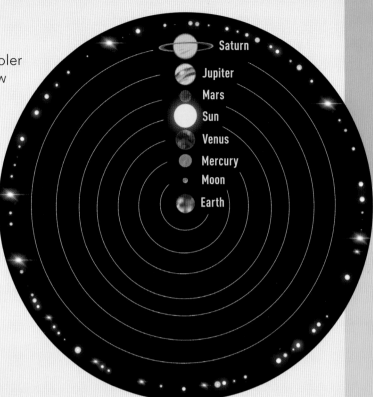

The Ptolemaic model of the solar system had Earth in the middle and the other bodies, including the Sun, in orbit around it

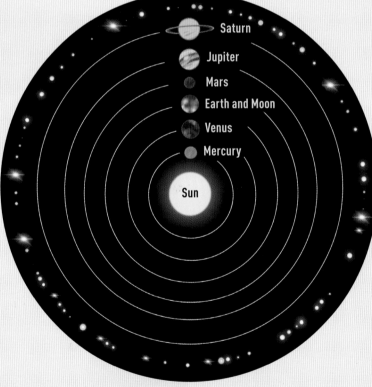

Copernicus's model of the solar system had the Sun in the middle and the other planets in orbit around it

SEEING MORE, SEEING FURTHER

More challenges came with the invention of the **telescope** in 1608 and its improvement by Galileo (see page 63). He saw that the surface of the Moon is pitted with craters, that the other planets are disks, not points of light, and that some of the planets even have moons of their own. The Milky Way, through a telescope, was clearly a band of stars, hugely increasing the number of stars the universe seems to hold and opening it up to be unimaginably vast.

1600–1649

In this period, European scientists began to understand more of the physical forces and energies around us, such as magnetism, light, and heat. They thought more, too, about what science is. The 1600s were the start of a golden age of science, with advances in many different areas.

1600

In England, William Gilbert explained **magnetism** in relation to the compass and Earth's magnetic field.

1606

In Italy, Giambattista della Porta noted the **heating effect of light**.

1603

German astronomer Johannes Kepler figured out how the **eye** focuses light and how **glasses** work.

1609

Johannes Kepler showed that the planets go around the Sun on **elliptical paths**.

1610

English thinker Francis Bacon noticed that the coasts of **West Africa and South America fit together**, buthe couldn't explain why.

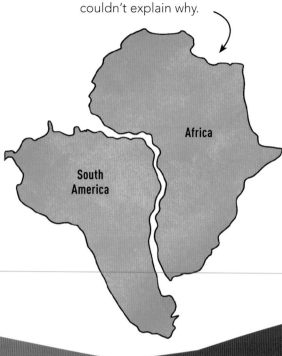

Africa

South America

1600

1614

Italian scientist Santorio Santorio ended 30 years of using a special device that weighed everything going into and out of his body. Doing this, he used **quantitative methods** (those that use numbers and quantities) in biology for the first time. He found he didn't excrete as much as he ate, but that most of the mass of his food and drink escaped as he sweated and breathed.

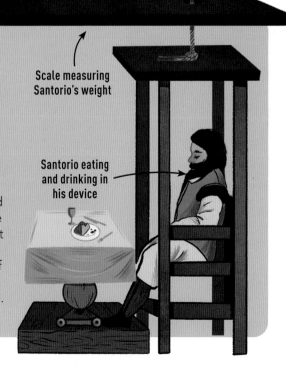

Scale measuring Santorio's weight

Santorio eating and drinking in his device

1619

Plague doctors in France wore cloaks and masks intended to protect them from catching the disease. The "beak" shape was filled with sweet- or strong-smelling substances such as lavender.

Galileo Galilei
1564–1642

Galileo was one of the most important **physicists and astronomers** of all time. His work on forces showed that a pendulum always swings at the same speed, that friction works to keep things from moving, how to calculate the path of a cannonball, and that the mass of an object doesn't affect how fast it falls. Hearing about the telescope, he made a better one. He saw the moons of Jupiter, rings of Saturn, craters on the Moon's surface, that the planets are other worlds, and that the Milky Way is made of stars. He was imprisoned for teaching the heliocentric model of the solar system.

1620

Francis Bacon outlined the **scientific method** followed by all modern scientists. He taught that a scientist should begin with a question or prediction (called a hypothesis), conduct investigations, and then test the hypothesis against the results.

1644

In Italy, Evangelista Torricelli demonstrated that air has mass, showing how **air pressure** works. He was the first person to create a **vacuum**—a space with no air or other substance in it.

1628

English surgeon William Harvey explained the **circulation of the blood**.

1637

French mathematician René Descartes described the **x/y coordinate system** used in graphs, said to have occurred to him after watching a fly in his room. He realized that he could state its position as distances from the edges of the walls.

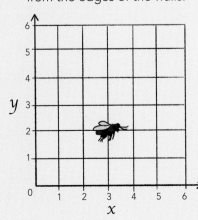

BEFORE 1644

Dutch chemist Jan Baptist van Helmont grew a willow tree in a pot, weighing the soil at the beginning and again after five years. Finding that the tree increased in weight by more than the weight lost by the soil, he concluded that **a plant grows mostly from water**. In fact, it also takes gas from the air.

Water added to small willow

Willow grows, but soil weighs nearly the same

SEEING FAR AND NEAR

Lenses are pieces of curved glass that change the path of light. They can be used to make things look nearer or more distant, and even to focus light and heat to start a fire. Single lenses have been used to magnify objects for a long time, at least since the time of the Ancient Greeks. In the 1590s, people began putting lenses together to gain greater magnification, making the first microscopes. It was a short step from magnifying small things nearby to making the first telescopes and so viewing larger things far away.

A telescope reveals the stars in the Milky Way

DUTCH LENS-MAKERS

The first **microscopes** were made in Holland around 1590. It's not very clear who invented the microscope, but it was probably either Hans Lippershey or father-and-son team Hans and Zacharias Janssen. These early microscopes consisted of a tube with a lens at each end. The lens near the object, called the objective lens, produced a magnified image that fell on a lens near the eye, called the eyepiece. The eyepiece magnified it again. The early microscopes gave magnification of up to 9x.

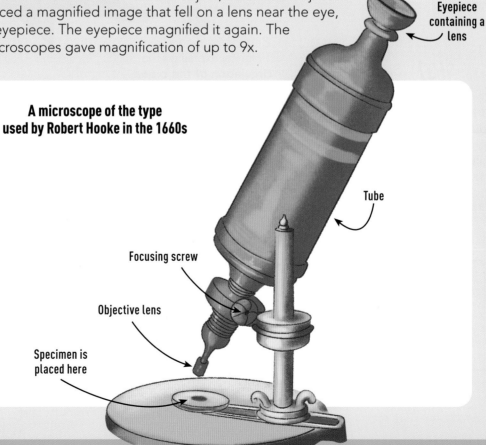

Eyepiece containing a lens

A microscope of the type used by Robert Hooke in the 1660s

Tube

Focusing screw

Objective lens

Specimen is placed here

STARING INTO SPACE

Using the same principle, the **telescope** was invented in 1608, very possibly by Hans Lippershey. Galileo improved it the next year and turned it toward the stars. Before this, it had mostly been used to look at distant objects on Earth, although the English astronomer Thomas Harriot had already made the first drawing of the Moon seen through a telescope. Galileo used his telescope to make important discoveries in astronomy.

In 1611, Johannes Kepler used the same kind of lens for both objective and eyepiece, making the telescope much better, and in 1668 Isaac Newton added a mirror, so that the eyepiece could be mounted on the side of the tube.

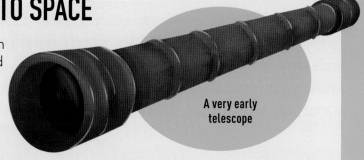

A very early telescope

A reflecting telescope

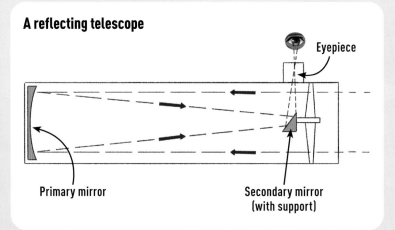

Eyepiece

Primary mirror

Secondary mirror (with support)

Drawn through the telescope

Galileo was the first person to make detailed drawings of objects in space seen through a telescope.

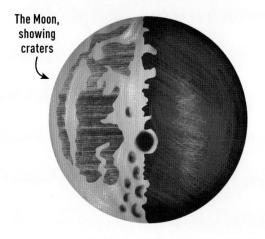

The Moon, showing craters

Galileo's picture of some of Jupiter's moons. They looked like stars through his telescope, but moved around and sometimes behind Jupiter.

In each row, the asterisks are the moons, and the circle represents Jupiter.

* * ○ *

○ * * *

* * ○

AN UNSEEN WORLD IN MINIATURE

The microscope revolutionized people's understanding of the world in the seventeenth century. In 1665, Robert Hooke improved the design greatly and could see and draw the structures of snowflakes, details of the bodies of tiny animals such as fleas, and the cells that make up the bodies of all plants and animals.

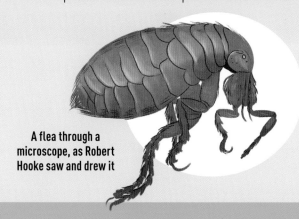

A flea through a microscope, as Robert Hooke saw and drew it

Soon after, in the 1670s, the Dutch microscopist Antonie van Leeuwenhoek made tiny, single-lens microscopes that he used to investigate body fluids and pond water, among other things (see page 65). Although his microscopes had only one lens, they could magnify up to 270x. Using them, he discovered the first microorganisms and saw some human cells, including red blood cells and sperm. He saw bacteria in the plaque from his own teeth and tiny protozoans in water from a pond. While the telescope had revealed worlds beyond our own, the microscope revealed untold miniature wonders within our own world.

1650–1699

In the second half of the seventeenth century, scientists in Europe continued to make great discoveries. The instruments that had been made earlier in the century opened up new ways of thinking about the natural world. People also began to explore things that cannot be touched or even seen, such as sound, light waves, and the idea of a vacuum.

1654

German physicist Otto von Guernicke demonstrated a **vacuum pump** and sucked the air out of two metal hemispheres. With the air removed, 16 horses could not separate the halves, as air pressure outside the hemispheres pushed them together.

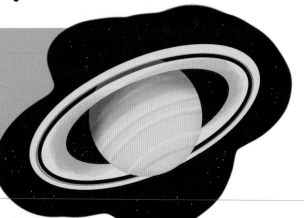

1656

In Holland, Christiaan Huygens discovered that the strange shapes Galileo had seen near Saturn were **rings around the planet**.

1665

English microscopist Robert Hooke published *Micrographia*, showing many objects through a microscope and naming cells, the tiny structural units that make up all living things.

1650

1656

Christiaan Huygens made the first **pendulum clock**.

1668

In Italy, Francesco Redi showed by experiment that **maggots come from fly eggs**, not directly from meat. He put meat in three jars, one open, one sealed, and one covered with mesh. Flies could not get into the sealed or covered jars and there were no maggots in them, but they could get into the meat in the open jar and maggots later appeared in it.

1666

Isaac Newton split white light into a **spectrum** and soon discovered that the spectrum can be put back together into white light. This was the first step toward recognizing the electromagnetic spectrum.

1669

Italian geologist Nicolas Steno noticed how **layers of rock** (strata) are laid down:

• The oldest are below more recent layers.

• Layers form horizontally but can be disrupted later.

• Layers start off being continuous over an area of land.

• If something cuts across a layer, it must have formed after the layer.

Steno stated that fossils are the remains of once-living organisms, while most people thought they grew in rocks.

Rock strata with fossils

1687

Isaac Newton published his *Principia*, explaining the laws of motion and the law of universal gravitation. It was one of the most important science books ever published.

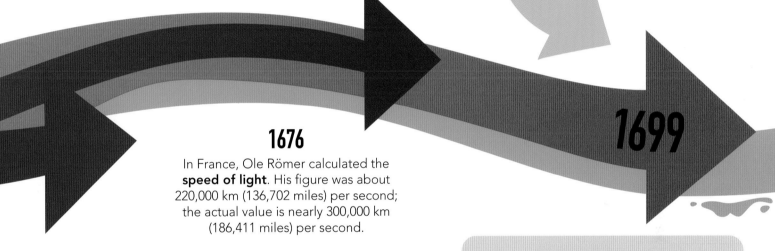

1676

In France, Ole Römer calculated the **speed of light**. His figure was about 220,000 km (136,702 miles) per second; the actual value is nearly 300,000 km (186,411 miles) per second.

1699

1672

Otto von Guernicke reasoned that **space is a vacuum** and that if we could climb up through Earth's atmosphere, we would eventually leave the air behind.

1676–1677

English botanist Nehemiah Grew showed that **plants have different tissues and structures**, just as animals do.

1683

Dutch lens-maker Antonie van Leeuwenhoek was the first person to **see bacteria** with microscopes of his own design.

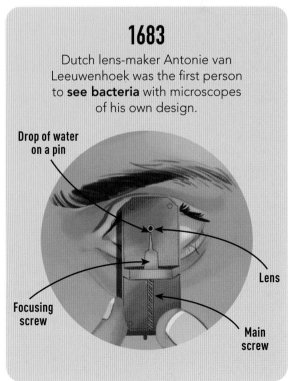

Drop of water on a pin

Lens

Focusing screw

Main screw

1676

English naturalist Robert Plot described and drew a large bone that had been brought to him. It is the first recorded **dinosaur bone**, although Plot thought it came from a giant human.

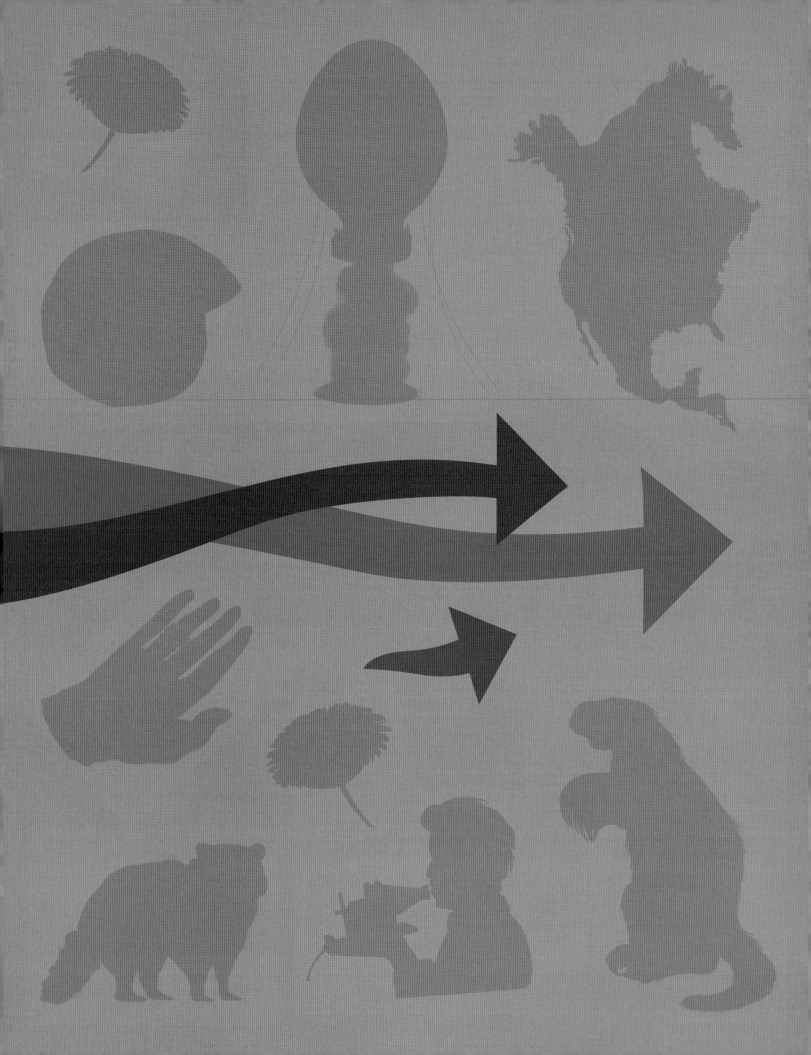

CHAPTER 4

BEYOND THE VISIBLE

The eighteenth and nineteenth centuries in Europe saw a blossoming of science. Religious explanations of the world were finally challenged, and people began to trust in humankind's ability to understand the universe through science. Discoveries that contradicted religious texts—such as Earth orbiting the Sun, Earth being very old, and evolution changing organisms over long periods—became acceptable in Europe and the United States.

During this period, Europe was at the heart of scientific progress. Science reached beyond what could be seen and measured to include the unobservable: atoms, radioactivity, thermodynamics, electricity, and diseases. Great technological developments brought changes to the everyday lives of many people in the West, with factories, trains, and steamships, and the wealth of consumer goods these brought to people who could afford them.

1700–1749

The eighteenth century continued the so-called "Age of Reason" begun in the seventeenth century, a time of confidence in science. As more and more discoveries were made, science began to split into different areas. Scientists started to specialize in an area such as physics or botany (plant science), rather than being generalists with wide-ranging interests.

1702

In France, Guillaume Amontons proposed **"absolute zero,"** the lowest possible temperature. From his work with gases, he noticed that pressure and temperature drop together. He then figured out that there must be a minimum temperature at which there would be no pressure. He set the figure at -240°C; the true figure is -273°C.

Émilie du Châtelet
1706–1749

Émilie du Châtelet was a French physicist and mathematician. She translated Newton's work into French in a version that is still used today. She was the first person to explain the concept of energy and to show the **conservation of energy**—how energy can't be created or destroyed. She predicted what is now known as infrared radiation and figured out the relationship between the energy, mass, and speed of an object from an experiment dropping cannonballs into wet clay and comparing the dents they made.

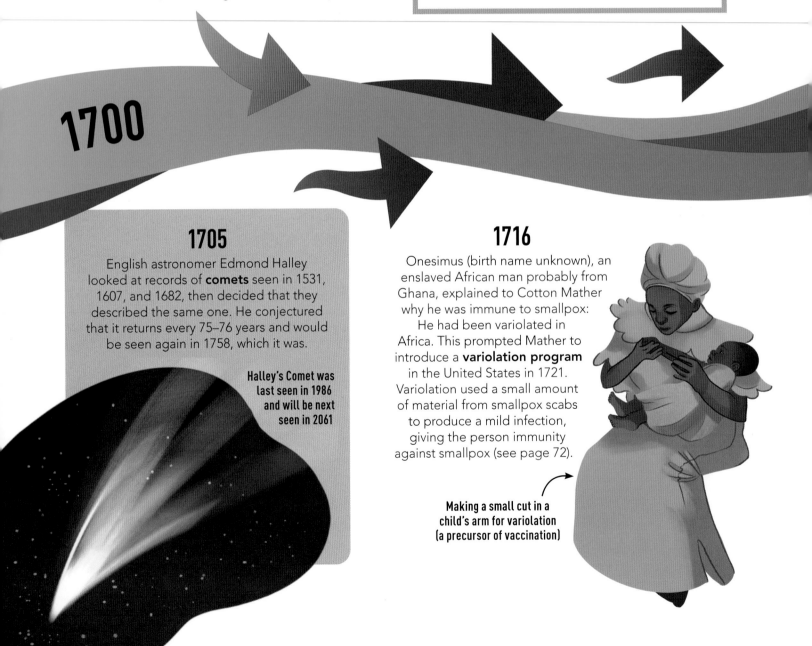

1700

1705

English astronomer Edmond Halley looked at records of **comets** seen in 1531, 1607, and 1682, then decided that they described the same one. He conjectured that it returns every 75–76 years and would be seen again in 1758, which it was.

Halley's Comet was last seen in 1986 and will be next seen in 2061

1716

Onesimus (birth name unknown), an enslaved African man probably from Ghana, explained to Cotton Mather why he was immune to smallpox: He had been variolated in Africa. This prompted Mather to introduce a **variolation program** in the United States in 1721. Variolation used a small amount of material from smallpox scabs to produce a mild infection, giving the person immunity against smallpox (see page 72).

Making a small cut in a child's arm for variolation (a precursor of vaccination)

1729

English astronomer Stephen Gray showed that **electricity** can flow through some substances (conductors) but not others (insulators). His demonstration involved charging a boy with static electricity, so that flecks of gold leaf leapt up to stick to his hands.

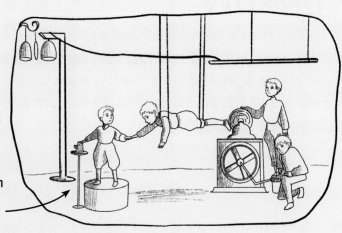

Demonstration of conduction of electricity using an unfortunate boy suspended from the ceiling

Bee pollinating a dandelion flower

1721

English botanist Philip Miller described **insects pollinating flowers**.

1747

Swedish naturalist Carl Linnaeus noted that dead animals **decompose** in the soil, enriching it, and their chemicals are **recycled** into growing plants (which other animals eat).

1727

In England, Stephen Hales suggested that plants take nutrients from the air and possibly use sunlight. This is the basis of **photosynthesis**, though he did not describe it fully. In 1754, Charles Bonnet showed that plants produce a gas (oxygen) in sunlight.

1749

1738

Swiss physicist Daniel Bernoulli discovered that fast-flowing fluids (liquids and gases) exert less pressure than slow-flowing fluids. This principle is central to **fluid dynamics**.

Digitalis purpurea
(common foxglove)

Salmo trutta
(brown trout)

Procyon lotor
(common raccoon)

1735

Carl Linnaeus **classified living things** using two-part names, giving a genus and species. For example, a tiger is called *Panthera tigris*, the first part showing it's a big cat and the second specifying a tiger. He was the first scientist to treat humans as just another type of animal, named *Homo sapiens*.

1750–1799

The final years of the eighteenth century were particularly important in chemistry, with the discovery of some important gases and the fact that oxygen is essential to life. Evidence began to appear that life on Earth had not always been the same and that Earth itself was older than people had thought.

Antoine Lavoisier

1743–1794

Working with his wife Marie-Anne Pierrette Paulze Lavoisier, the French chemist Antoine Lavoisier began modern **chemistry**. He stated that matter can't be destroyed or created, that we breathe in oxygen and breathe out carbon dioxide, that oxygen is needed for things to burn, and that water consists of hydrogen and oxygen. He also made the first list of chemical elements (substances that can't be broken down).

1752

French chemist René Antoine Ferchault de Réaumur showed that **digesting food is a chemical process**. He fed a bird with meat in a metal tube attached to a string. When he pulled the tube back up the bird's throat, the meat was partly digested, but the tube was undamaged, showing that chemicals, not mechanical crushing, caused digestion.

Réaumur retrieved the metal tube containing part-digested meat from the bird's stomach

1750

1752

American scientist Benjamin Franklin showed that **lightning is electric** by flying a kite in a thunderstorm with a metal key attached to the string. Electricity from the air was conducted by a metal rod on the kite, through a wet string to the key. Touching the key, Franklin experienced a shock.

1772

English chemist Joseph Priestley showed that mice and burning candles need a gas produced by plants. A mouse died in a jar containing a burning candle, but if he also put a plant in, the mouse survived. In 1774, he discovered the gas needed is **oxygen**.

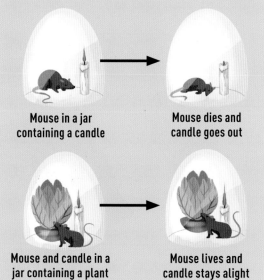

Mouse in a jar containing a candle

Mouse dies and candle goes out

Mouse and candle in a jar containing a plant

Mouse lives and candle stays alight

1783

Joseph-Michel and Jacques-Étienne Montgolfier launched the first **hot-air balloon**, soaring 900 m (½ mile) above Paris, France. It flew 5.6 km (3 ½ miles) in 25 minutes.

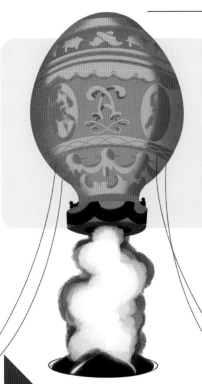

1778

In France, Georges-Louis Leclerc declared that **Earth is more than 70,000 years old**. He said the planet had cooled from hot molten rock, and rain formed the oceans.

1796

Edward Jenner developed the first **vaccine**—against smallpox (see pages 72–73).

1785

English geologist James Hutton argued that Earth is very old and that **geological processes** are still slowly going on, with erosion, earthquakes, and volcanic eruptions reshaping Earth's surface over millions of years.

1799

1779

In England, Jan Ingenhousz discovered that **leaves give out oxygen** in sunlight but carbon dioxide in darkness.

1781

In England, William Herschel discovered **Uranus**, the first planet to be identified since ancient times.

1796

French naturalist Georges Cuvier proved that some animals have gone **extinct**, showing that mastodons (giant elephants) and megatheriums (giant ground sloths) had once lived in the Americas.

Mastodon

Megatherium

1799

Alessandro Volta made the first **electric battery** from a pile of alternating disks of copper and zinc separated by cardboard or cloth soaked in salt water.

VACCINATION

Edward Jenner produced the first vaccine in England in 1796, eventually leading to smallpox being wiped out. Smallpox caused fever, aches, pains, and a rash that covered the body with small boils. Many sufferers died, and others were left blind or horribly scarred. At its height, smallpox killed one in twelve people around the world. Vaccination was not the first method for helping people become immune to disease.

A patient with smallpox

A LITTLE PUFF

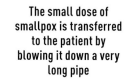

An earlier practice called **variolation** was used in China, India, and later Africa, possibly starting as early as 200 BCE in China. One method was to grind up matter from the scabs of someone who had smallpox and blow it into the patient's nostril. Another method involved putting pus or scabs from smallpox sores in a little cut in the patient's skin. The small dose encouraged the patient's immune system to produce antibodies that would protect them in the future, but it was quite dangerous.

In variolation, the patient receives smallpox matter through a nostril, and they begin making protective antibodies

The small dose of smallpox is transferred to the patient by blowing it down a very long pipe

MOVING WEST

Onesimus was variolated as a child in Africa

Lady Mary Wortley Montagu

Variolation was introduced into America by Cotton Mather and an enslaved African known as Onesimus, and in Europe by Lady Mary Wortley Montagu.

Onesimus taught Mather about the process in 1716, and Mather had it used during a smallpox epidemic in 1721. The first anti-vax movement was against variolation in the 1720s.

A BETTER WAY

Edward Jenner, an English country doctor, noticed that milkmaids who had the related disease cowpox never developed smallpox. Jenner collected pus from cowpox sores and used it to inoculate a young boy. The boy developed a mild cowpox illness. Jenner then deliberately exposed the boy to smallpox—an experiment that would not be allowed now—but the boy didn't get sick. Jenner began to vaccinate other people, giving them protection against smallpox. He, too, was ridiculed and abused by anti-vaxxers, but vaccination spread quickly as a safe alternative to variolation.

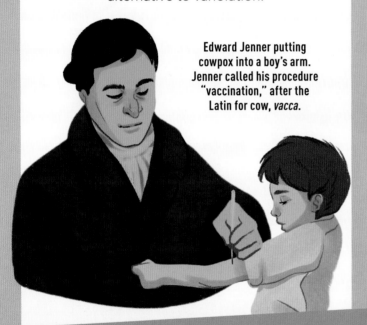

Edward Jenner putting cowpox into a boy's arm. Jenner called his procedure "vaccination," after the Latin for cow, *vacca*.

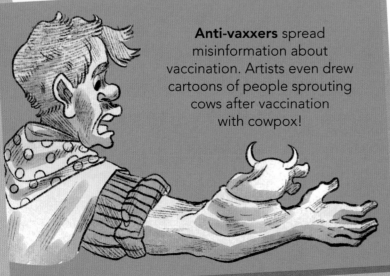

Anti-vaxxers spread misinformation about vaccination. Artists even drew cartoons of people sprouting cows after vaccination with cowpox!

MORE VACCINES

The next important vaccine was for rabies, developed by **Louis Pasteur** and used from 1885. He tested it first on dogs and then on a boy who had been bitten by a rabid dog and had not yet developed rabies. The boy survived—the first rabies patient (assuming he actually had the disease) to live. Vaccines for other diseases followed, and the process gradually changed from using live microbes to using those that had been made inactive when possible. These could not produce the disease, only prompt the body to make antibodies for it. Vaccination has saved tens of millions of lives.

Louis Pasteur

Dimorphodon

1800–1824

The nineteenth century began with new discoveries about Earth's distant past. Fossils of unfamiliar types of animals came to light—flying reptiles and reptiles that swam in the sea, and then the first dinosaur. These suggested that the world had once been very different.

1803

English chemist John Dalton stated that all matter is made of tiny particles called **atoms** that can't be split apart, created, or destroyed. The mass and size of atoms is different for each of the chemical elements. Chemical reactions involve moving atoms around and combining them in different ways to make **compounds**. This idea became the basis of modern chemistry.

Mary Anning
1799–1847

Mary Anning began collecting **fossils** as a child with her brother and father. The family had a small business selling fossils in Dorset, England, which Mary took over in the 1820s. Mary and her brother found several major fossils, including ichthyosaurs and plesiosaurs (both marine reptiles), and the first pterosaur found outside Germany: Dimorphodon. Anning became an expert paleontologist, but her work was under-recognized because she was a woman.

1800

1801

In a famous experiment, English physicist Thomas Young showed that **light behaves like waves**. Light that is passed through two slits makes a pattern of light and dark bands, as waves passing through the slits spread out and cross each other. This contradicted Newton's idea that light is made of particles.

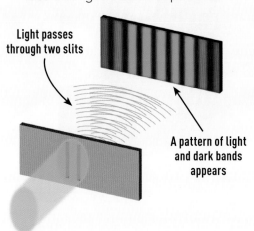

Light passes through two slits

A pattern of light and dark bands appears

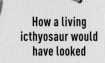

How a living icthyosaur would have looked

1811

Joseph and Mary Anning found the fossilized skeleton of a large **ichthyosaur**, leading paleontologists to recognize that large marine reptiles lived in the distant past.

1804

Swiss chemist Nicolas-Théodore de Saussure found that plants take **carbon** from the atmosphere and probably take **hydrogen** from water, combining these as their source of food.

Fossilized head of an icthyosaur

BEYOND THE VISIBLE

Dark lines break up the spectrum of sunlight. These are now called Fraunhofer lines

1814

German chemist Joseph von Fraunhofer rediscovered **dark lines in the spectrum** of sunlight and the light from stars, first seen in 1802. He thought that information about the chemicals in stars and the Sun could be discovered from these lines, though he couldn't do this himself (see page 77).

1816

French doctor René Laënnec invented a simple wooden **stethoscope** to listen to the chest of his patients. As a musician who carved flutes, he had the skills needed to make a wooden tube that worked as a stethoscope.

Laënnec using his carved wooden stethoscope to listen to a boy's breathing

1820s

French chemist Joseph Fourier recognized that **gases** in Earth's atmosphere must **trap the Sun's heat**, keeping the planet a stable temperature.

1824

1815

The fossilized bones of an unknown animal found in Oxfordshire, England, were sent to William Buckland at the University of Oxford. He named this extinct creature *Megalosaurus* in 1824—the **first dinosaur** ever named.

Megalosaurus with detail of lower jawbone

1821

In England, Michael Faraday discovered that a changing electric field produces a magnetic field, and vice versa. This became the basis of the **electric generator**.

1822–1832

English inventor Charles Babbage designed the first **mechanical computer**, which he called a Difference Engine. The mathematician Ada Lovelace wrote the instructions for it, which is considered to be the first computer program. Babbage had hoped to automate the many long and complex calculations needed for navigating (plotting a course) at sea. The calculations took a long time, and people made mistakes. His invention would have calculated them accurately and quickly, but Babbage couldn't make his machine at the time. It was finally built in 1991.

1825–1849

The nineteenth century was an important age for chemistry, as people came to understand more about the substances that make up our world and beyond. One of the most important discoveries of this period was that the chemical ether could be used as an anesthetic. By putting people to sleep, it made surgical operations possible and was the first step toward safe modern medicine.

1840

American John Draper took the first **photograph of the Moon**.

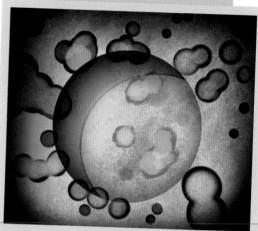

1827

While looking at pollen grains with a microscope, Scottish botanist Robert Brown saw tiny particles jostling around but couldn't explain them. Einstein later showed that they are moved by molecules of water colliding with them, proving the existence of **atoms**.

1830–1833

Charles Lyell published *Principles of Geology*, which set out the basis of modern **geology**. He saw that the processes that have shaped Earth are still going on, including rocks building up as soil and sand being deposited by rivers and worn away by wind and water.

1825

1831

Charles Darwin set sail on HMS *Beagle* for a journey around the world, on which he collected plants and animals and made notes on rocks that supported Lyell's view of geological processes. His observations later led to his **theory of evolution** (see page 80).

A giant tortoise from the Galápagos Islands

1840

German chemist Justus von Liebig worked on plants' need for nitrogen, phosphorous, and potassium. He suggested using artificial **fertilizer** to supply chemicals missing from the soil.

1839

Work in Germany by Theodor Schwann on animals and Matthias Schleiden on plants revealed that all living things are made of **cells**, and these are the building blocks of life.

1842

English naturalist Richard Owen **named dinosaurs**. Only three had been discovered: Megalosaurus, Iguanodon (now called Mantellisaurus), and Hylaeosaurus. Owen recognized that they were all part of a group of very large, extinct reptiles.

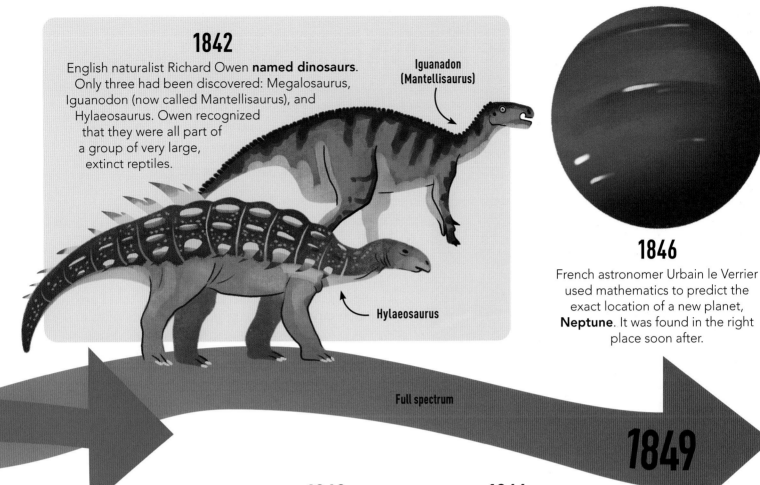

Iguanadon (Mantellisaurus)

Hylaeosaurus

Full spectrum

1846

French astronomer Urbain le Verrier used mathematics to predict the exact location of a new planet, **Neptune**. It was found in the right place soon after.

1849

1843

English physicist James Joule discovered that **heat is the result of atoms moving**, and so is mechanical. Previously, people thought of heat as a kind of substance called "caloric," which was mixed into other matter, making it hot.

1846

American dentist William Morton used ether as an **anesthetic** in a public demonstration, removing a tumor (growing lump) from the neck of an unconscious patient. This led to a revolution in surgery, which previously had been very painful and difficult.

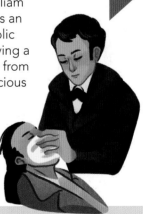

Ammonite fossil

1841

English geologist John Phillips suggested splitting Earth's geological history into three major eras, the **Paleozoic, Mesozoic, and Cenozoic**, divided by clear changes in the fossils found. He used fossils to figure out which were the oldest rock strata, and roughly outlined the ages of fish, then reptiles, then mammals and birds, and finally humans.

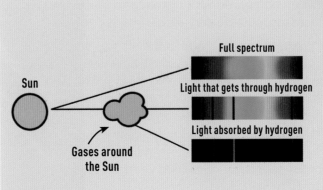

Full spectrum

Sun

Light that gets through hydrogen

Light absorbed by hydrogen

Gases around the Sun

C. 1849

German chemists Robert Bunsen and Gustav Kirchhoff explained the Fraunhofer lines in the spectrum of sunlight as showing wavelengths of light absorbed by the Sun's own atmosphere. From this, they could identify elements in the Sun (see page 80).

EARTH'S LONG HISTORY

For millennia, people have wondered how Earth began and how old it is. In 1654, the Irish clergyman James Ussher calculated the age of Earth by adding together the ages of people mentioned in the Bible and came up with a date of 4004 BCE for Earth's creation. At first, any challenges to this "young Earth" model caused outrage in the Christian West.

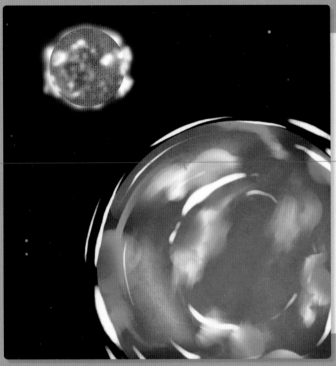

Sun and Earth in space

OLDER THAN YOUNG

As geology became a science, it seemed that **Earth was much older**. The first scientific estimate of its age came in 1779. Georges Leclerc made a scale model of Earth, heated it to a temperature he thought matched that of the newly formed planet, and timed it cooling. He figured out that Earth would have taken 75,000 years to cool to its current temperature. This was much longer than the age Ussher had calculated, but still far short of Earth's real age of 4.5 billion years. Leclerc wasn't the first to suggest an old Earth. The Russian naturalist Mikhail Lomonosov had already suggested that Earth might be over hundred thousand years old.

FROM THOUSANDS TO MILLIONS

When Hutton described the forces and processes that shape the land in 1785, he assumed that these took place at the same rate as now. We can't see the landscape changing much, even when compared with historical records, so the processes must be very slow.

More estimates of the **age of Earth** made in the nineteenth century used different methods, including how long people thought the Sun could continue to glow (so Earth must be younger than that), and how long it would take the sea to accumulate its salt. In 1862, the physicist William Thomson found that it would take an Earth-sized ball of completely molten rock between 24 and 400 million years to cool. He later reduced this to 100 million years and then to 20 million years.

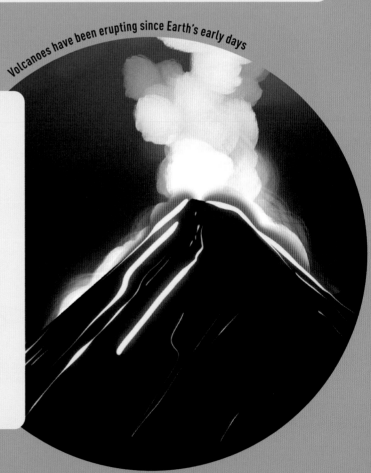

Volcanoes have been erupting since Earth's early days

LIFE AND ROCKS

Darwin's work on evolution suggested that a few million years would not be long enough for all living things to evolve. Biologists and physicists argued over how old Earth might be, but geology brought life and rocks together in **fossils**. The discovery of the fossils of dinosaurs and other extinct animals showed that there had been time for completely different and strange kinds of life to evolve and then disappear. Fossils lying in different layers could help geologists to date rocks relatively—to say which were older than others—but did not give an absolute age for them. That would have to wait for the later discovery of radiometric dating, which uses the radioactive content of rocks to give a date for their formation. Even when people accepted that living things had changed over time, there was no way of judging how quickly they changed—just that it was too slow to show up in recorded history.

Fossilized bones of Plesiosaurus and how it would have looked swimming

1850–1874

Several world-changing discoveries belong to this period. The theory of evolution and the realization that there is a whole spectrum of types of electromagnetic radiation came within a few years of each other, changing science forever.

1852 and 1855

In Germany, Robert Remak and Rudolf Virchow stated that all cells are produced from preexisting cells, which divide. This is the basis of modern **cell theory**.

1859

Robert Bunsen and Gustav Kirchhoff made the first **spectroscope** to find out what the Sun is made of. The dark bands in the spectrum of sunlight are caused by chemical elements in the Sun absorbing light of some wavelengths. By identifying the elements that absorb those wavelengths, they showed which elements are present in the Sun.

Spectrum showing three of the Sun's elements

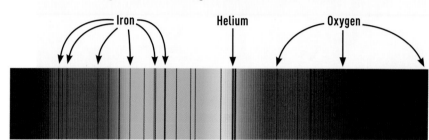

Iron   Helium   Oxygen

1850

As Earth turns below it, the pendulum swings between different points on the marked circle

1856

In America, Eunice Foote identified carbon dioxide and water vapor as **greenhouse gases**. She predicted that rising levels of carbon dioxide would produce **global warming**.

1859

French biologist Louis Pasteur **disproved spontaneous generation** (the idea that living things can come from nonliving matter). He showed that if microbes are killed by boiling a flask of broth and further microbes can't enter the flask, no microbes will appear in it.

1858–1859

English naturalists Charles Darwin and Alfred Russel Wallace published **theories of evolution** at the same time, in 1858. Darwin then published a full book in 1859, *On the Origin of Species*, which is one of the most important scientific books ever published. He explained that organisms change over time (evolve) or become extinct, depending on how well suited they are to their environment. He couldn't explain how evolutionary changes come about.

1851

Using a giant pendulum, French physicist Léon Foucault proved that **Earth rotates on its axis**. The pendulum always swings in the same direction, but as the ground turns below it, the pendulum points to different places marked on a large circle below.

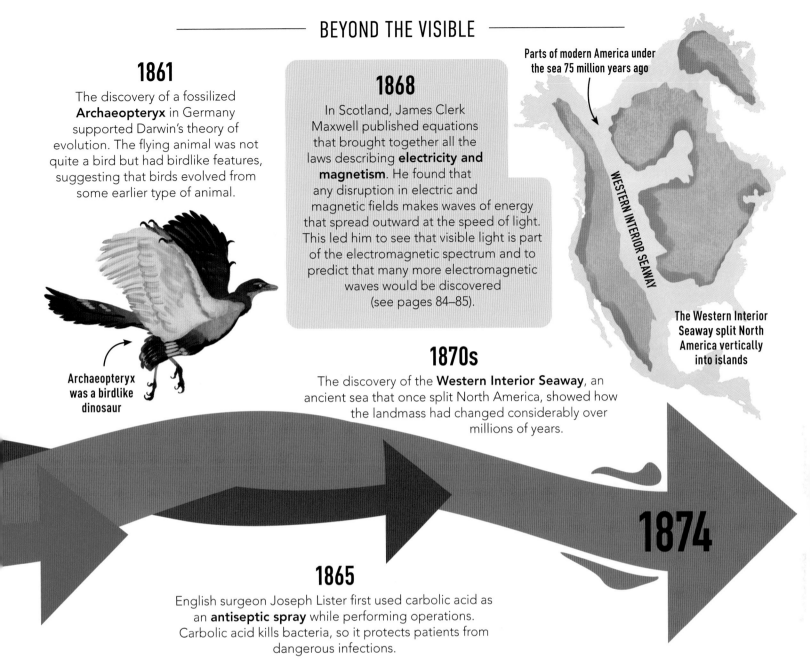

1861

The discovery of a fossilized **Archaeopteryx** in Germany supported Darwin's theory of evolution. The flying animal was not quite a bird but had birdlike features, suggesting that birds evolved from some earlier type of animal.

Archaeopteryx was a birdlike dinosaur

1868

In Scotland, James Clerk Maxwell published equations that brought together all the laws describing **electricity and magnetism**. He found that any disruption in electric and magnetic fields makes waves of energy that spread outward at the speed of light. This led him to see that visible light is part of the electromagnetic spectrum and to predict that many more electromagnetic waves would be discovered (see pages 84–85).

Parts of modern America under the sea 75 million years ago

WESTERN INTERIOR SEAWAY

The Western Interior Seaway split North America vertically into islands

1870s

The discovery of the **Western Interior Seaway**, an ancient sea that once split North America, showed how the landmass had changed considerably over millions of years.

1874

1865

English surgeon Joseph Lister first used carbolic acid as an **antiseptic spray** while performing operations. Carbolic acid kills bacteria, so it protects patients from dangerous infections.

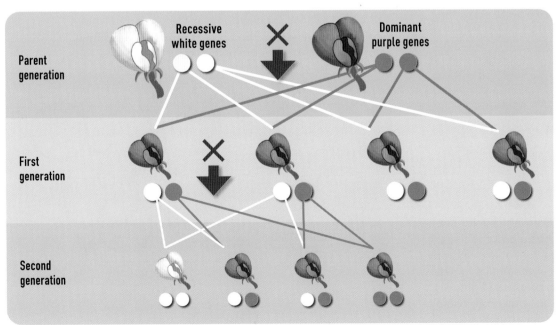

Parent generation — Recessive white genes × Dominant purple genes

First generation ×

Second generation

1866

Gregor Mendel published the results of his experiments with breeding peas, which he started in 1856. He described **inheritance** in terms of paired characteristics, with one of each pair usually dominant over the other.

1875–1899

The end of the nineteenth century saw more discoveries among things that can't be seen—the waves of energy that make up the electromagnetic spectrum and viruses too small to see with the microscopes available. Some of the discoveries of previous decades began to be put to use in inventions that have since become everyday objects.

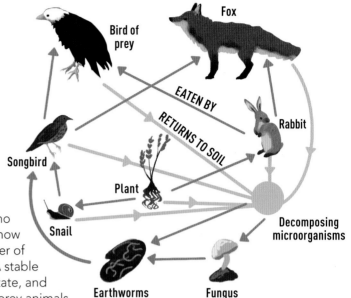

1876

Discovering the bacteria that cause anthrax, German biologist Robert Koch showed that a particular germ always causes the same disease—the basis of germ theory.

1880

In Italy, Lorenzo Camerano explored **food webs** and how predators keep the number of prey animals in balance. A stable balance is the natural state, and there are never so many prey animals that they eat all the available plants and begin to starve. He perhaps produced the first diagram of a food web, which shows how organisms depend on each other for food.

1875

1876

Alexander Graham Bell invented a **telephone**, putting to use information that scientists had discovered about how sound waves work. This was the first step in the telecoms (telecommunications) revolution that brought all modern communication methods.

1879

Thomas Edison's development of the **light bulb** put to use the link between heat and light: By heating a wire until it glows, the bulb produced light. His was the first practically useful light bulb.

1882

German biologist Walther Flemming saw through a microscope how the normal body cells of organisms make copies of themselves. He named the process **mitosis**. This is how bodies grow and repair themselves.

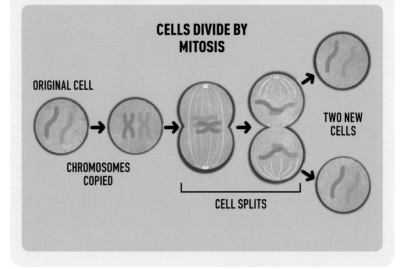

CELLS DIVIDE BY MITOSIS

ORIGINAL CELL

CHROMOSOMES COPIED

CELL SPLITS

TWO NEW CELLS

1883

The volcanic island **Krakatau** erupted catastrophically, killing everything living on the island. This gave biologists the chance to watch an ecosystem reestablish from nothing.

1897

English physicist J. J. Thompson discovered the **electron**, the first subatomic particle to be found.

Marie Skłodowska Curie
1867–1934

Born in Poland, Maria Skłodowska moved to France where she worked as a chemist. With her husband Pierre Curie, she worked on radioactivity. They discovered two new radioactive elements, polonium and radium, in 1898, and Marie pioneered the use of **radiotherapy**—the medical use of radioactivity. During World War I, she and her daughter set up mobile X-ray units to help treat wounded soldiers.

1896

French chemist Henri Becquerel discovered **radioactivity**, finding that uranium emits energy without having to store it up, by being exposed to light or heat.

1898

In Holland, Martinus Beijerinck discovered **viruses**. He found that a liquid extracted from plants infected with tobacco mosaic virus could infect healthy plants, even after passing through a filter fine enough to remove bacteria.

1896

In Austria, Sigmund Freud used **psychoanalysis** to treat patients with mental illness. This involved talking to them and understanding their mental state from what they said, remembered, and had dreamed.

1899

1883

The Belgian biologist Edouard van Beneden saw **meiosis** in the eggs of a roundworm. This is how egg and sperm cells are created, each with half the material needed to make a new organism.

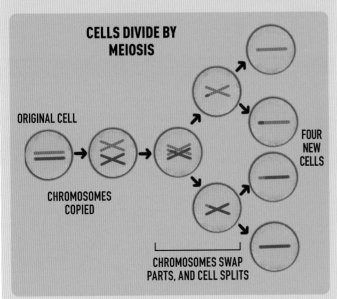

CELLS DIVIDE BY MEIOSIS

ORIGINAL CELL

CHROMOSOMES COPIED

FOUR NEW CELLS

CHROMOSOMES SWAP PARTS, AND CELL SPLITS

1888

German physicist Heinrich Hertz demonstrated that he could create **radio waves**. When asked what they might be useful for, he answered, "Nothing, I guess."

1895

In Germany, Wilhelm Röntgen discovered **X-rays**. He found that he could make an image of bones or metal objects hidden from view within material that the "rays" could penetrate.

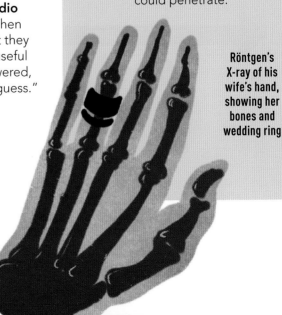

Röntgen's X-ray of his wife's hand, showing her bones and wedding ring

WAVES OF ENERGY

The nature of light and other types of energy baffled scientists for years. When Isaac Newton discovered that sunlight could be split into a spectrum, matching the rainbow, light suddenly looked a lot more complicated than it had done before.

A SPECTRUM FROM WHITE

Before Newton, people knew that light could be split by a glass prism, but thought that the spectrum could be seen because the light had been corrupted (spoiled) in the glass. In 1666, Newton passed a spectrum through a second prism, recombining it into white light to show that this wasn't the case. His explanation was that white light is composed of **particles**, which he called "corpuscles" of different colors. When combined, these produced white light.

PARTICLES OR WAVES?

Not everyone believed that light was made of particles. Some thought it was **waves**. Thomas Young's double-slit experiment in 1801 (see page 74) showed that light does, in fact, behave like a wave. It produces interference patterns when passed through slits, just as waves in the sea show interference patterns when the sea passes through narrow channels and then comes together again.

Splitting white light with a glass prism

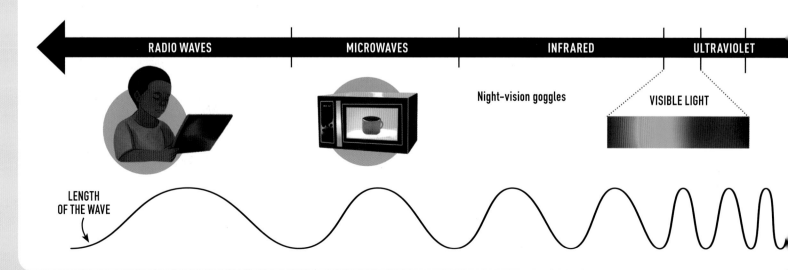

The electromagnetic spectrum

RADIO WAVES   MICROWAVES   INFRARED   ULTRAVIOLET

Night-vision goggles

VISIBLE LIGHT

LENGTH OF THE WAVE

MORE WAVES

In 1800, the astronomer Frederick William Herschel split sunlight into a spectrum and measured the temperature of different colors of light. He found that the temperature increased from violet to red, and the highest temperature was recorded by a thermometer placed beyond the red band. He announced the discovery of "calorific rays." We call them **infrared**. The next year, Johann Ritter experimented at the other end of the spectrum with chemicals that react in sunlight and discovered **ultraviolet**. This showed that not all "light" is visible.

BEYOND LIGHT

James Clerk Maxwell was interested in what seemed to be different waves: those produced by electricity and magnetism. He showed that any disturbance in electric and magnetic fields produced waves of energy that spread outward. In 1873, he showed that light was part of the same group of waves. So, too, were infrared and ultraviolet. His work suggested that electromagnetic waves could exist at any frequency. Some of these new types of waves began to be discovered soon after: **radio waves** in 1886, **X-rays** in 1895, and **gamma rays** in 1900.

A FULL SPECTRUM

We now know that there are many types of electromagnetic energy that travel as waves, all at the speed of light. The **wavelength** of the energy sets its properties and how we experience it. Energy with a large wavelength (a large distance between the peaks of waves) is radio waves, while visible light has shorter wavelengths. X-rays and harmful gamma-ray radiation have very short wavelengths. The electromagnetic spectrum underpins all modern communication methods. Parts of the spectrum are put to other specific uses, too, such as microwaves for cooking, X-rays for looking inside bodies, and radiation for cancer treatments.

The satellites that gives us GPS, pinpointing a location on Earth, use radio waves

The **electromagnetic spectrum** is the full spectrum of radiation—of waves of energy with different wavelengths. We use different types of energy for different things, from communications to looking inside bodies or at distant stars.

X-RAYS   GAMMA RAYS

Cancer treatment

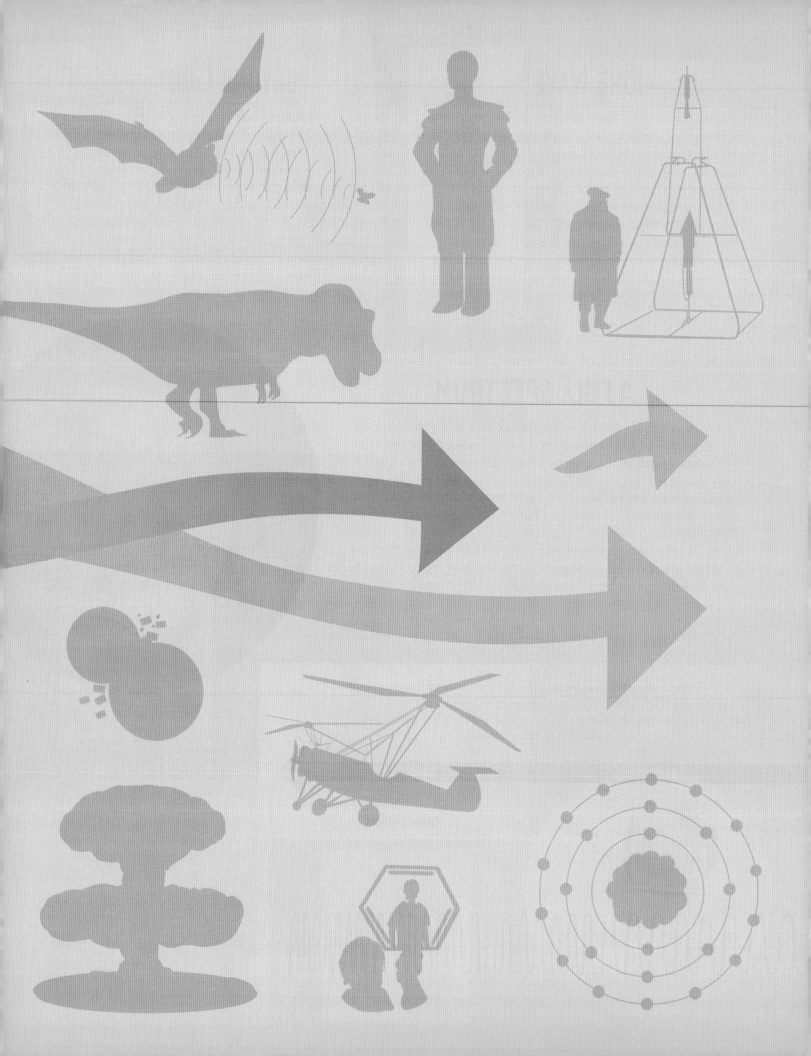

CHAPTER 5

REBUILDING THE WORLD

The first two-thirds of the twentieth century saw the beginning of what many people think of as the modern scientific age. In this period, scientists unpicked the chemistry of life itself and came to understand the structure of the atom—and how devastating amounts of energy could be released from it. They saw the vastness of the universe, and gained antibiotics and other treatments that revolutionized medicine. Europe and the United States were often at the forefront of scientific advances. The most exciting science of all was the Moon landing, right at the end of the period. With it, humankind finally broke free from this planet and took the first step on the path to exploring other places in space.

1900–1909

The world started the new century in a spirit of optimism and confidence. Progress came quickly in many different fields. In theoretical science (that which is not immediately put to practical use), physics began a revolution that would reshape our understanding of matter, energy, and forces. The work of Albert Einstein and the beginnings of quantum physics set physicists on a new path.

1900

German physicist Max Planck stated the basis of **quantum physics**: that energy always exists in parcels of fixed sizes called "quanta." This seemed to contradict the idea of light existing as waves. Light is now thought to behave as both waves and particles.

Albert Einstein

1879–1955

German physicist Albert Einstein is considered one of the greatest scientists of all time. He discovered the photoelectric effect, which lies behind how solar panels work, he proved the existence of atoms, and he presented two **theories of relativity**. The theory of special relativity gives a new way of thinking about motion, especially at very high speeds. It suggests that space and time are a single thing, spacetime, and that matter and energy are interchangeable. His theory of general relativity describes gravity as a feature of spacetime, with spacetime curving where gravity is strongest.

1900

1900

Making the same discoveries as Mendel on inherited characteristics, Dutch botanist Hugo de Vries suggested that inherited characteristics change when a **mutation** occurs—a mistake in copying genetic information. This is how a species acquires new features, driving evolution.

1900

In Germany, Karl Landsteiner discovered the **blood groups** A, B, and O. This made blood transfusions possible, since a person's body can only deal with blood of a compatible blood group.

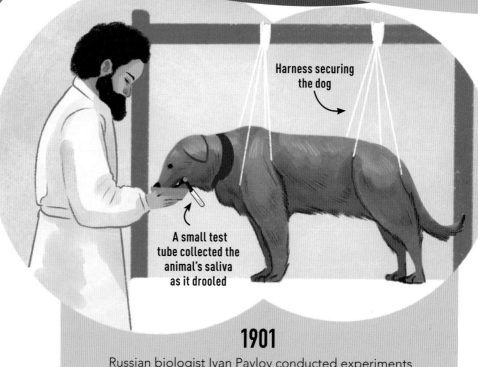

Harness securing the dog

A small test tube collected the animal's saliva as it drooled

1901

Russian biologist Ivan Pavlov conducted experiments with dogs, training them to link particular noises with being fed. After some time, the dogs' mouths would water just at the noise, even if no food arrived. Pavlov called this a **conditioned reflex**.

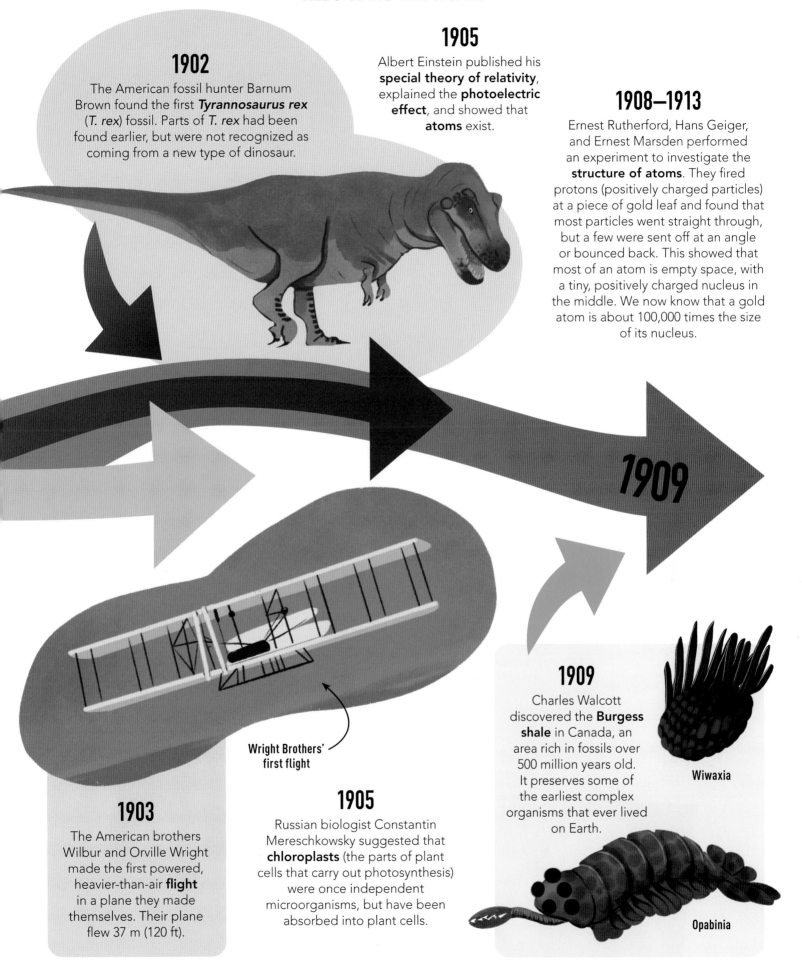

1902

The American fossil hunter Barnum Brown found the first *Tyrannosaurus rex* (*T. rex*) fossil. Parts of *T. rex* had been found earlier, but were not recognized as coming from a new type of dinosaur.

1905

Albert Einstein published his **special theory of relativity**, explained the **photoelectric effect**, and showed that **atoms** exist.

1908–1913

Ernest Rutherford, Hans Geiger, and Ernest Marsden performed an experiment to investigate the **structure of atoms**. They fired protons (positively charged particles) at a piece of gold leaf and found that most particles went straight through, but a few were sent off at an angle or bounced back. This showed that most of an atom is empty space, with a tiny, positively charged nucleus in the middle. We now know that a gold atom is about 100,000 times the size of its nucleus.

1909

Wright Brothers' first flight

1903

The American brothers Wilbur and Orville Wright made the first powered, heavier-than-air **flight** in a plane they made themselves. Their plane flew 37 m (120 ft).

1905

Russian biologist Constantin Mereschkowsky suggested that **chloroplasts** (the parts of plant cells that carry out photosynthesis) were once independent microorganisms, but have been absorbed into plant cells.

1909

Charles Walcott discovered the **Burgess shale** in Canada, an area rich in fossils over 500 million years old. It preserves some of the earliest complex organisms that ever lived on Earth.

Wiwaxia

Opabinia

89

1910–1919

While physicists and astronomers made good progress in the period 1910–1919, World War I and a worldwide flu pandemic hindered much science in the second half of the decade.

1915

Albert Einstein published his **general theory of relativity**, explaining gravity as curvature in spacetime.

1912

American astronomer Henrietta Swan Leavitt studied a type of star that grows brighter and dimmer at regular intervals, sending out **more or less light energy**. From the speed of pulsing, she could conclude which stars were farthest away.

1913

Danish physicist Niels Bohr found that **positive charge** in an atom is located in a dense nucleus and the **electrons** orbit around it in fixed "shells."

Electron

Dense nucleus

1910

1912

Polish biochemist Kazimierz Funk discovered that **vitamins** are a vital part of our diet.

1912

German weather scientist Alfred Wegener suggested that the **continents slowly move** around the surface of Earth. His evidence was that the coasts of South America and Africa fit together well, and that identical fossils are found in lands that are now very far apart.

South America and Africa moving apart as the Atlantic Ocean opens

1915

Spinosaurus, the largest known meat-eating dinosaur, was described from a fossil dug up in Egypt in 1912. Spinosaurus lived 112–97 million years ago and ate fish.

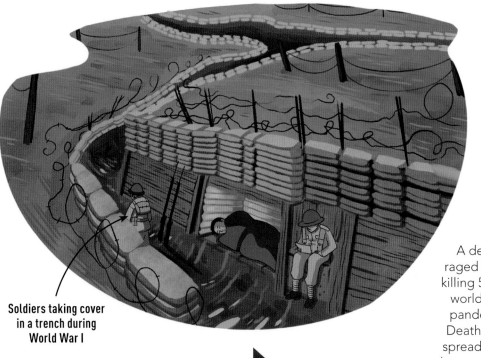

Soldiers taking cover
in a trench during
World War I

World War I preoccupied most countries in the world during 1914–1918. The most terrible war that had ever been fought, it was the last to see horses in action and the first to see tanks, aircraft, aerial bombing, and poison gas.

1918

A deadly **flu pandemic** raged from 1918 until 1921, killing 50–100 million people worldwide. The deadliest pandemic since the Black Death, it was probably first spread by soldiers returning home around the world after fighting in World War I.

1919

1917

A photograph of the spectrum of a star taken with the Mount Wilson telescope in California, USA is probably the first evidence ever found of an **exoplanet** (a planet outside our solar system). It wasn't identified as indicating an exoplanet until 2007.

1919

John Alcock and Arthur Brown made the first **nonstop transatlantic flight**, flying from Newfoundland in Canada to County Galway in Ireland in just under 16 hours. They won a prize of £10,000 that had been offered by a British newspaper before the start of World War I.

1919

American astronomer Harlow Shapley discovered that the **Sun** is not at the middle of the galaxy but about **two-thirds of the way out**.

1919

Arthur Eddington proved that **gravity bends light**, showing that Einstein's general theory of relativity is correct. He did this by comparing photos taken around the world during a solar eclipse with photos taken before the eclipse. This revealed that the apparent position of a star behind the Sun doesn't match its actual position because its light is bent by the Sun's gravity.

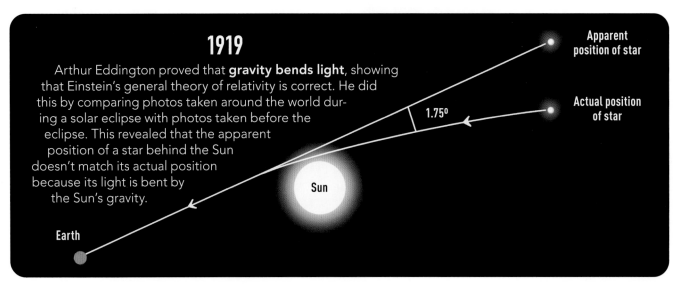

Apparent position of star

Actual position of star

1.75°

Sun

Earth

1920–1929

As the world made its slow recovery from World War I and the flu pandemic that followed, there was little time or money for large-scale science. Important work came from small, cheap projects and work with existing equipment.

1920

In a "Great Debate" in the United States, leading astronomers discussed whether the fuzzy objects known as **nebulae** are objects inside the Milky Way or other galaxies beyond it (see page 94).

1920

American psychologists John Broadus Watson and Rosalie Rayner conducted a cruel experiment on a baby, training him to become frightened of a white rat and other furry objects. They did this by making a loud noise with a hammer when showing him the rat and other objects. This proved that **humans could be conditioned** in the same way as Pavlov's dogs (see page 88).

Experimenters used a hammer hitting a pipe to make a loud noise

1920

1924

American astronomer Edwin Hubble announced that the nebula **Andromeda** is another galaxy. This meant that the universe is much larger than astronomers had thought (see page 95).

1920

Astronomer Andrew Douglass started examining **tree rings** to find out about the climate in the past. The activity of the Sun, which affects Earth's weather, changes how quickly trees grow, so they lay down thicker or thinner rings of growth each year.

Tree rings inside a cut tree trunk

1923

The first fossils recognized as **dinosaur eggs** were discovered, preserved in the dry sand of the Gobi Desert, Mongolia. The dinosaurs that laid them were Oviraptors, a small, speedy dinosaur that ran on its hind legs.

1920

The Czech play *R.U.R.* (*Rossum's Universal Robots*) introduced the word **robot** and showed robots as automated, mechanical, humanlike figures. This triggered a desire to build actual robots.

Nest of Oviraptor eggs

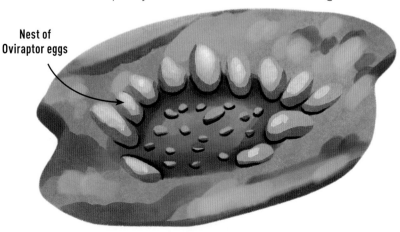

1925

Scottish engineer John Logie Baird developed a **television** that showed black and white moving images. He showed it in public the following year, starting the age of television.

1925

English-American astronomer Cecilia Payne-Gaposchkin showed that stars are made almost entirely of the gases **hydrogen and helium** (see page 95).

1929

American astronomer George Gamow suggested that the stars, including the Sun, produce their heat and light by **fusing hydrogen atoms into helium**.

1929

1927

Belgian astronomer Georges Lemaître suggested that the universe had expanded from an infinitely tiny point. This later became known as the **"Big Bang" theory** of the origin of the universe (see page 95).

1928

Scottish doctor Alexander Fleming discovered that **penicillin**, a substance produced by a kind of fungus, could kill the bacteria that caused various infections. He found this by accident, after going away without clearing away his experimental work. He had grown bacteria on plates of special jelly and left them in his laboratory. On his return, he found that patches of his bacteria had been killed by mold growing on the plates.

1926

American physicist Robert Goddard launched the first **liquid-fueled rocket**. It reached a height of only 13 m (42 ½ ft) on a flight lasting two seconds, but it set the scene for the rocket technology that has powered space flight.

Fleming's penicillium growing in the middle of a plate of bacteria

Bacteria killed by penicillium

1929

American astronomer Edwin Hubble showed that the **universe is still expanding**.

THE UNIVERSE EXPANDS

People first studied nebulae—fuzzy patches of light—in the night sky in the eighteenth century. In the 1920s, astronomers discovered that many nebulae are galaxies far beyond our own.

THE GREAT DEBATE

In 1920, George Ellery Hale organized a debate between two great American astronomers to try and decide what **spiral nebulae** are. Harlow Shapley argued that the nebulae were objects inside the Milky Way, which he believed to be much larger than astronomers had previously thought. He calculated that the solar system is not near the middle of the Milky Way, and that the entire galaxy is 300,000 light years across. Heber Curtis argued that the nebulae are "island universes"—other galaxies outside the Milky Way. He believed our galaxy to be only 30,000 light years across, with the Sun near the middle.

**OUR GALAXY,
THE MILKY WAY**

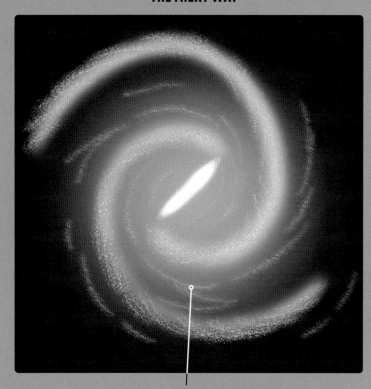

The solar system lies between two main spiral "arms" of the Milky Way, not near the middle

In 1774, the French astronomer Charles Messier made the first list of nebulae, which became known as Messier objects. Some are now known to be galaxies, while others are clusters of stars, dust clouds, or supernova remnants.

MANY GALAXIES

The question was finally settled in 1924 by Edwin Hubble. Using the largest telescope in the world, he could see stars inside the spiral nebula Andromeda, supporting the idea that it's a **galaxy**. He then used a method that measures the brightness of a special type of star in it to calculate that Andromeda is 900,000 light years away—it's actually even more distant: Two million light years away. This put it outside the Milky Way, even using the largest estimates for the size of the galaxy. Hubble's stunning conclusion was that the universe is much larger than anyone had ever imagined and contains many galaxies.

Andromeda spiral galaxy

GROWING AND GROWING

Another American astronomer, Vesto Slipher, showed in 1925 that most nebulae seem to be moving away from Earth at great speed. If all galaxies are roughly the same size, those which look smallest must be farthest away. The Belgian astronomer Georges Lemaître found that the nebulae that look smallest (so are most distant) are moving fastest. Since most nebulae are becoming more distant, that suggests the universe is expanding. Lemaître pointed out that if the universe is expanding, it must once have been much smaller, even very tiny. He described a single point, or "primeval atom," which expanded into the current universe. We now call this the **"Big Bang" theory**.

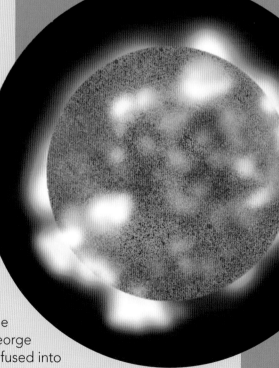

LOOKING LOCALLY

While Hubble concentrated on the universe, Cecilia Payne-Gaposchkin worked on an individual star, the Sun. She calculated in 1925 that it is made almost entirely of the gases **hydrogen and helium**. In 1929, George Gamow showed that hydrogen could be fused into helium within a star.

The Sun

By the end of the 1920s, astronomers had figured out that the universe contains many galaxies, it is expanding from its origins as a tiny point, and its energy could be produced by stars fusing hydrogen.

1930–1939

In the period between the two world wars, most countries put more effort into rebuilding and recovering than into new science. Even so, progress in astronomy continued, as well as in developments related to war, such as radar, and energy from breaking apart atoms.

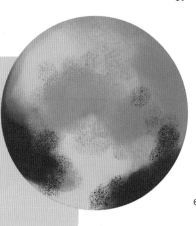

1930

American amateur astronomer Clyde Tombaugh discovered **Pluto**, then considered a planet but now downgraded to a dwarf planet.

1931

American scientists Harry Wood and Frank Neumann developed the **Modified Mercalli Intensity Scale** to report the severity of earthquakes. It is based on seeing and assessing the effects of an earthquake, such as damage to buildings or feeling the ground shaking.

1933

Swiss astronomer Fritz Zwicky calculated that galaxies are moving too fast for the mass that astronomers thought they had. This means there must be some invisible matter that we don't see but that adds mass to them. He called this **"dark matter."** We still don't know what it is.

1930

1931

American engineer Karl Jansky accidentally picked up radio waves from space. This led him to make the first **radio telescope** in 1932. Radio telescopes pick up radio waves, instead of light, from distant stars and other objects.

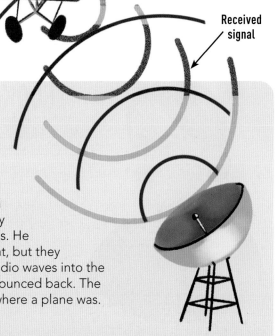

Transmitted signal

Received signal

1930

The first **golden hamsters**, ancestors of all modern pet hamsters, were collected near Aleppo, Syria.

1935

Radar was first used to detect aircraft. Scottish engineer Robert Watson-Watt had been asked to find a way to destroy enemy aircraft with radio waves. He said it was impossible to do that, but they could be spotted by sending radio waves into the sky and looking for any that bounced back. The reflected waves would show where a plane was.

1935

English botanist Arthur Tansley described the idea of an **ecosystem** as a community of living things that interact with each other and their environment.

A freshwater ecosystem consisting of plants, waterbirds, fish, and insects

1938

In Germany, Konrad Zuse finished making the first electrically powered **mechanical computer**, the Z1. The machine and the plans for it were destroyed in a bombing raid during World War II.

1939

American physicists J. Robert Oppenheimer and Hartland Snyder predicted **black holes**. They suggested that a dying star might collapse into itself, becoming so dense that not even light can escape the pull of its gravity.

1936

Danish physicist Inge Lehmann discovered that Earth has a **solid inner core**.

1936

The first practical **helicopter**, the German Focke-Wulf Fw 61, made its first flight.

1936–1937

British mathematician Alan Turing developed the idea of a "Turing machine," as it's now known. This **general-purpose computer** could be programmed to do a wide variety of tasks (as modern computers can). In 1950, he would propose a test for whether a computer should be considered intelligent, now called the Turing test.

1938

A **coelacanth**, a type of fish thought to have been extinct for 65 million years, was recognized by museum worker Marjorie Courtenay-Latimer on a fishing boat in South Africa.

1939

German physicists Otto Hahn and Lise Meitner found that the vast amount of energy released when uranium atoms are broken apart using high-speed neutrons is converted from mass. This is **nuclear fission**—the source of energy for atomic weapons and atomic power plants.

1940–1949

World War II dominated the 1940s. Most of the science from this decade was involved with the war effort—developing computers and weapons. But there was also a theory about how the Moon formed and a new way of measuring the age of really old objects.

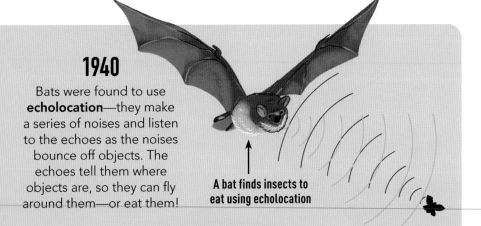

1940

Bats were found to use **echolocation**—they make a series of noises and listen to the echoes as the noises bounce off objects. The echoes tell them where objects are, so they can fly around them—or eat them!

A bat finds insects to eat using echolocation

World War II started in 1939 when Germany, under the Nazi dictator Adolf Hitler, invaded part of Poland. Agreements between countries to help each other brought more nations into the war. The Nazis wanted to take over parts of Europe and build a German "master race." This involved killing millions of people whom they believed to be inferior. It was the first war to be fought largely in and from the air, with cities devastated by bombs dropped by aircraft.

1940

1940–1941

English chemists Howard Florey and Ernst Chain made the antibiotic medicine **penicillin** from the mold Fleming had discovered in 1928 (see page 93). Penicillin saved hundreds of thousands of lives in World War II.

1941

German inventor Konrad Zuse demonstrated the Z3, the first working fully programmable **digital computer**.

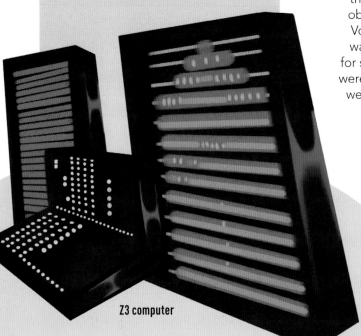

Z3 computer

1942

The **V2 rocket**, designed by Wernher von Braun in Germany, became the first human-made object to reach space. Von Braun's intention was to design rockets for space travel, but they were taken over to use as weapons during World War II.

1943

The first electronic programmable computer, **Colossus**, was built and operated in secret as part of the British war effort. It was destroyed after the war and remained a secret for many decades.

1946

American astronomer Reginald Daly suggested that a planet around the size of Mars, now called Theia, collided with Earth more than four billion years ago. All of Theia and part of Earth vaporized (turned to gas). A cloud of gas, dust, and rock orbited Earth until eventually the pieces clumped together to **form the Moon**.

1944

DNA was identified as the genetic material that enables organisms to inherit characteristics from their parents (see pages 100–101).

1947

Fruit flies became the first living things sent into space and returned alive, on a V2 rocket. They were sent to test whether radiation in space would make space travel too dangerous for humans to attempt.

1949

1947

An expedition sailed a wooden raft named **Kon-Tiki** across the Pacific Ocean from Peru to Indonesia, proving that it was possible for early people to have migrated from South America in this way. Their raft was made using only materials available thousands of years ago.

1949

American chemist Willard Libby first used the method of **carbon dating**— calculating the age of objects by examining the proportion of radioactive carbon they contain. He tested it on old objects of known date, including part of an object from the tomb of the Egyptian pharaoh Djoser.

1945

The US Air Force dropped two **atomic bombs** to force Japan's surrender in World War II. These were the first and only atomic weapons ever used outside tests. They caused devastating loss of life and damage.

Pyramid of Djoser

DECODING DNA

When Charles Darwin set out his theory of evolution in 1859, he had no idea how evolution might work. At around the same time, Gregor Mendel's experiments with peas revealed patterns in how features are inherited. In the twentieth century, scientists put the two together, discovering how inheritance and evolution work.

LIKE PARENT, LIKE CHILD

Inherited characteristics are coded in **chromosomes**, long strings of the chemical **DNA** (which stands for deoxyribonucleic acid). Each chromosome is split into **genes**, and an organism's combination of genes decides what it is like. For example, you might have genes for black hair or freckles. Chromosomes had been seen in the nucleus (middle) of cells in the 1860s, but no one knew what they did until 1902. Then, Walter Sutton and Theodor Boveri linked Mendel's work on inherited characteristics with chromosomes.

FRUIT FLIES AND GENES

The American geneticist Thomas Hunt Morgan demonstrated the link between chromosomes and inheritance. Morgan worked with fruit flies. They have a short life span and reproduce quickly, so he could breed many generations in a short time and see how features were passed on. Alfred Sturtevant worked with him to make the first **"gene map"** in 1913 showing which parts of a chromosome produced which features in an organism.

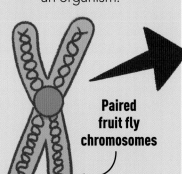

Paired fruit fly chromosomes

GENE MAP OF FRUIT FLY INHERITANCE
Mutations at the point on the chromosome shown by the stripes change features from those of normal flies (top row) to mutated flies (bottom row)

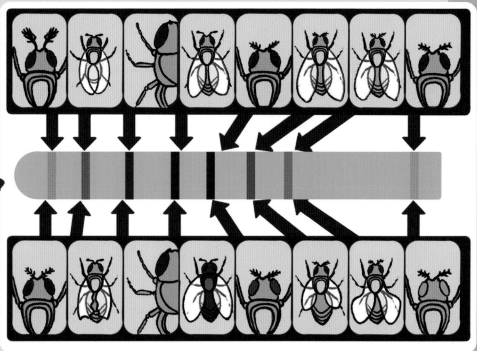

TIME FOR A CHANGE

In 1911, Thomas Hunt Morgan saw that **chromosomes cross over and mix their parts** during reproduction. Instead of inheriting a whole chromosome, the next organism gets some genes from each parent on each chromosome.

Morgan also showed how new features can be introduced. **Mutations** are mistakes made when chromosomes are copied. The mistakes sometimes give the organism useful features; at other times, the changes are harmful or make little difference to it. These changes can also be inherited, as long as they don't harm the organism so much that it can't breed. Mutations give a way for organisms to change in new ways, so provide a way for evolution to work. The discovery linked Darwin's theory with genetics.

HOW CHROMOSOMES CROSS OVER AND MIX THEIR PARTS

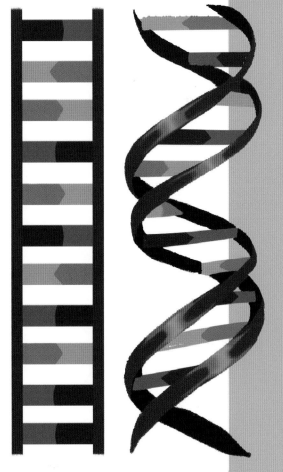

1
2
3
4

UNRAVELING DNA

Scientists still had to discover how the DNA molecule carried information. The answer came in 1953. Francis Crick and James Watson, working from photographs taken by Rosalind Franklin, figured out that DNA is a **double helix**, something like a ladder twisted into a spiral.

The genetic information is coded into the pattern of rungs between the two uprights of the ladder. Each rung is made of a pair of chemicals. There are only two possible pairs, but they can be swapped left to right, making a total of four possible arrangements. Hundreds or thousands of rungs make up a gene, so there are many possibilities.

Discovering the structure of DNA allowed people to find out how it could carry genetic information as a code

Rosalind Franklin took a photo of a DNA molecule that was the vital clue

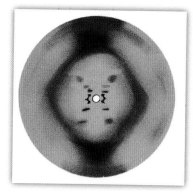

The photo shows DNA end on— so looking down into the spiral

1950–1959

After World War II, scientists returned to exploring space and the natural world. The discovery of how landmasses slowly move around Earth's surface and of fossils older than any previously discovered began to reveal the early history of our planet.

1950

Dutch astronomer Jan Oort proposed the **Oort Cloud**, a thick shell of icy chunks surrounding the solar system. Some chunks are the size of mountains or larger, and there are billions or even trillions of them. They form a ball around the solar system, stretching a quarter or halfway to the next nearest star. The Oort Cloud is the home of long-period comets—those that are seen from Earth only once every few hundreds or thousands of years.

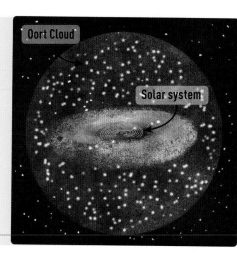

Oort Cloud

Solar system

1953

American biologists Stanley Miller and Harold Urey showed that some of the organic molecules essential to life can be created from **inorganic chemicals** in conditions they believed were present on early Earth. This showed that life could have started on Earth, given the right chemical ingredients and a source of energy.

1953

Francis Crick, James Watson, and Rosalind Franklin described the **structure of the DNA molecule**, explaining how genetic inheritance works (see page 101).

1950

1950

German biologist Willi Hennig introduced the science of **cladistics**, classifying organisms by their common evolutionary history. Cladograms show where different types of organisms split from others as they evolved. Unlike a tree diagram, cladograms show all organisms as equal, suggesting none is more developed than others.

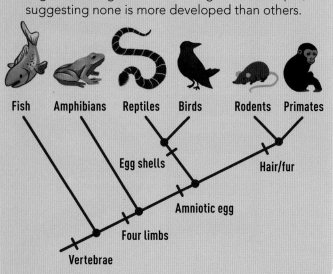

Fish Amphibians Reptiles Birds Rodents Primates

Egg shells

Hair/fur

Amniotic egg

Four limbs

Vertebrae

1952

English biologists Andrew Huxley and Alan Hodgkin showed that the **electric signals of nerves** are produced by chemical reactions.

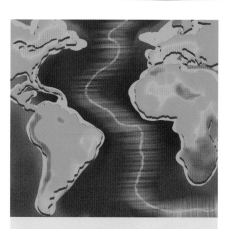

1952

A **mechanical heart** was used to keep a patient alive during heart surgery in the United States. The "heart" was outside the body, pumping the patient's blood for 50 minutes while his own heart was repaired. He lived another 30 years.

1953

The **Mid-Atlantic Ridge** was discovered. It's a deep-sea canyon bordered by mountains running north–south through the middle of the Atlantic Ocean. Along this line, parts of the Earth's crust (surface) pull apart, and new rock forms on the seabed.

1954

The first **solar-powered battery** was made in the United States. Solar power makes use of the photoelectric effect described by Einstein in 1905 (see pages 88 and 89), using sunlight to produce electricity.

1955

American Earth scientist Clair Patterson fixed the age of Earth as **4.55 billion years**.

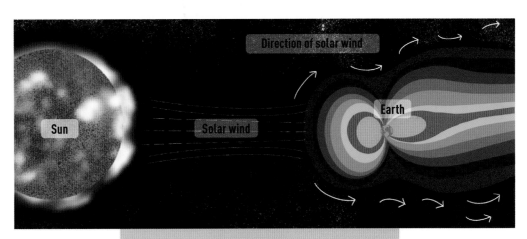

Direction of solar wind

Sun

Solar wind

Earth

1958

Earth's **magnetosphere** was discovered. It is a vast magnetic field around Earth that protects the planet from harmful radiation from the Sun. It ensures that the atmosphere is not ripped away by the solar wind.

1959

1957

The first **satellite**, Sputnik 1, was launched from the USSR. About the size of a beach ball, it took 98 minutes to orbit Earth. Sputnik remained in space for three months and sent radio signals to Earth for three weeks.

1957

English schoolboy Roger Mason discovered the fossilized organism Charnia, the **first fossil definitely older than 542 million years**.

1959

The spacecraft Luna 3, launched from the USSR, took the first photos of the **far side of the Moon**. This side always faces away from Earth, so it had never been seen before.

1960–1969

As much of the world finally recovered from World War II, a spirit of optimism and ambition drove incredible developments in science and technology. People wanted to make better lives and push the boundaries of what was possible—even venturing beyond Earth.

Rachel Carson

1907–1964

Rachel Carson was an American biologist who studied the **natural environment**. In 1962, Carson published a book called *Silent Spring*, which pointed out the huge damage done to the natural world by pesticides used to kill insects. She took on the powerful industries that made these harmful chemicals and fought successfully to reduce their use.

1965

American physicists Arno Penzias and Robert Wilson detected the **cosmic background radiation**, which had been predicted years earlier but never found. This leftover radiation from the start of the universe is the signature of the Big Bang (see pages 93 and 95).

1966

The Polish-American chemist Stephanie Kwolek developed **Kevlar**, a super-strong, lightweight material that is now used in many things, from engines to bulletproof vests.

1960

1960

American physicist Theodore Maiman built the first **laser** using a crystal of ruby. A laser focuses an extremely narrow beam of light energy that can be used like a knife or to make accurate measurements.

1960

Two dogs, named Belka and Strelka, became the **first large animals to survive orbiting Earth** in a spacecraft.

1961

Yuri Gagarin orbited Earth for 108 minutes in the tiny capsule Vostok 1. The **first human ever to go into space**, he became a national hero in the USSR.

1966

Luna 9, from the USSR, became the first spacecraft to achieve a **soft landing on the Moon**, rather than crash into it.

1960

Transplants between unrelated people became possible only after scientists had developed drugs to prevent the body from rejecting an organ from someone else. The first successful **human organ transplant** between unrelated individuals was of a kidney by John Hopewell in the UK.

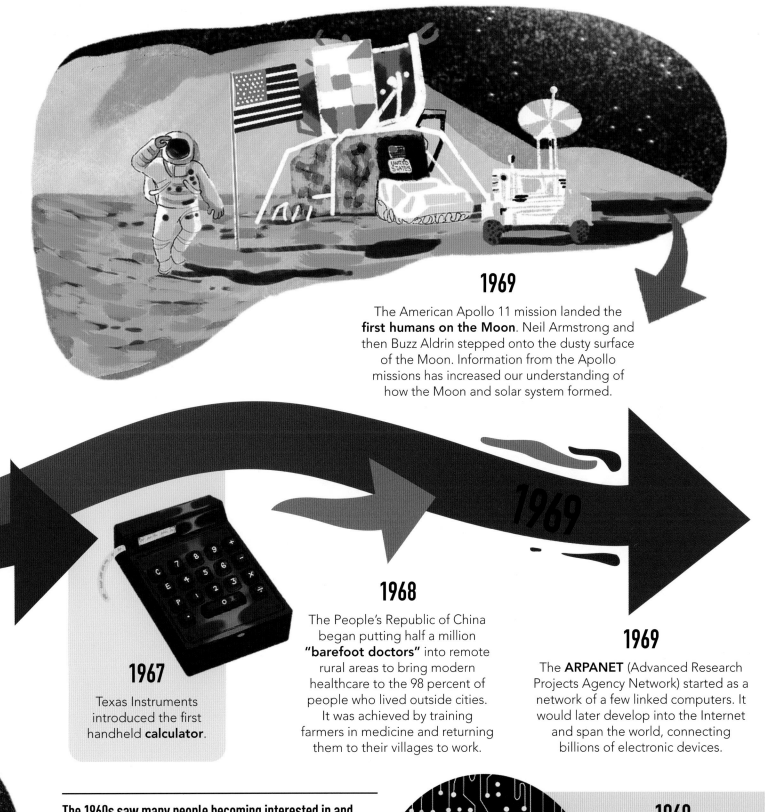

1969

The American Apollo 11 mission landed the **first humans on the Moon**. Neil Armstrong and then Buzz Aldrin stepped onto the dusty surface of the Moon. Information from the Apollo missions has increased our understanding of how the Moon and solar system formed.

1969

1967

Texas Instruments introduced the first handheld **calculator**.

1968

The People's Republic of China began putting half a million **"barefoot doctors"** into remote rural areas to bring modern healthcare to the 98 percent of people who lived outside cities. It was achieved by training farmers in medicine and returning them to their villages to work.

1969

The **ARPANET** (Advanced Research Projects Agency Network) started as a network of a few linked computers. It would later develop into the Internet and span the world, connecting billions of electronic devices.

The 1960s saw many people becoming interested in and worried about the natural environment for the first time. Starting with Rachel Carson's battle against pesticides, an environmentalist movement began that has grown into the current "green" movement to protect the environment from harm caused by human activities. The struggle between environmentalists and big business has expanded to many other areas beyond pesticides.

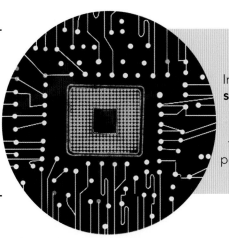

1969

Intel began work on the first **single-chip microprocessor**, the Intel 4004. This packed computing power onto a tiny sliver of silicon, making personal computers possible. It went on sale in 1971.

CHAPTER 6

STRETCHING THE BOUNDARIES

By the end of the twentieth century, science had largely lost its national boundaries and become truly international. Today, scientists from around the world work alongside one another, whether on the International Space Station orbiting Earth or in laboratories and field sites all over the world. International cooperation has become possible through the recent development of the Internet and the vast collection of smart, computerized equipment it links together. Our science can now go far beyond the limits of what any person or group could achieve, as it harnesses the power and intelligence of superfast computers for sequencing DNA, inventing new molecules, and churning through data at unimaginable speeds.

OUT OF THIS WORLD

Until the 1950s, space could only be explored using telescopes. But there are limits to what we can discover with Earth-based telescopes. By sending humans and robots into space and launching space-based telescopes that can see farther and in greater detail than those on Earth, we have found out much more about the universe.

A RACE IN SPACE

The first rocket to get into space was launched in 1942 by German engineer Wernher von Braun. It just went up and then down. In 1957, the Soviet satellite Sputnik became the first object to orbit Earth, and in 1961 Yuri Gagarin became the first person ever to go into space.

The launch of Sputnik triggered a **"space race"** with the USSR and the United States competing to reach new targets in space. Much of this focused on the Moon: The first craft to orbit around the Moon (Luna 10, 1966), the first landing on the Moon (by Luna 9, 1965), and finally the first humans to step on the Moon, achieved by Apollo 11 in 1969. But the Moon wasn't the only target. Space agencies in the USSR and the United States also sent probes to other planets. Probes are spacecraft with no crew, controlled from Earth. They fly around and sometimes land on other planets, also on asteroids and comets, sending back photographs and collecting data that could not be gathered from Earth.

SERIOUS ABOUT SPACE

Of all the planets, Mars has been visited most because it is most like Earth—although it is still very different. The first craft to land successfully on Mars was Viking 1 in 1976. Since then, there have been many more, some carrying rovers that can move around and collect data. The latest NASA rover, Perseverance, landed in 2021 to collect rock samples that should one day be picked up and returned to Earth.

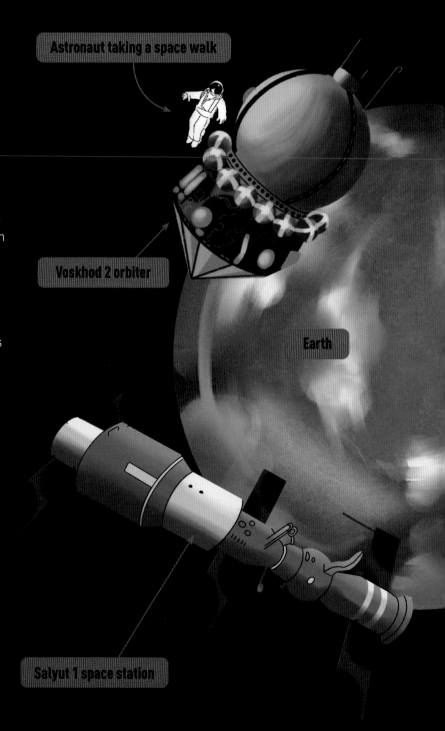

Astronaut taking a space walk

Voskhod 2 orbiter

Earth

Salyut 1 space station

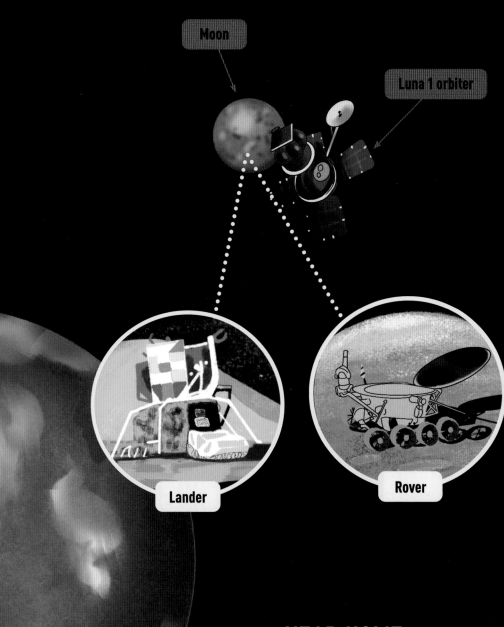

Moon

Luna 1 orbiter

Lander

Rover

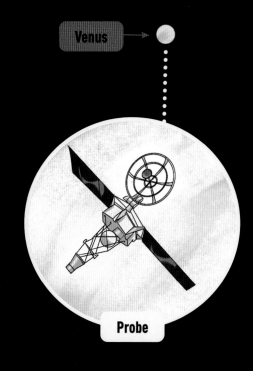

Venus

Probe

... AND FAR AWAY

One of the most ambitious space projects is also one of the oldest. The two **Voyager** craft, launched in 1977, have flown by several planets and have left the solar system to set off into interstellar space. Voyager 1 is now more than 22.5 billion km (14 billion miles) from Earth.

NEAR HOME ...

While some probes travel long distances, **space stations and satellites** stay close to Earth. The first space station was Salyut 1, launched in 1971. The only space station working now is the International Space Station (ISS), used by scientists from around the world to conduct experiments and investigations in space. Thousands of satellites orbit Earth, providing everything from phone signals to Google Earth images. Space telescopes, such as Hubble and the James Webb telescope, gain a clear view of space by being outside Earth's atmosphere.

1970–1979

The 1970s saw the first steps toward making computers much smaller and cheaper. At the same time, developments in space exploration continued. Soon, computers would play a more important part in space technologies.

1970

The first robotic **rover** landed on the Moon. Called Lunokhod 1 and launched from the USSR, it worked for 322 days, sending back thousands of photos and examining the regolith (surface dust and rock).

1974

The **"Arecibo message"** was broadcast into space. It is a picture sent as a radio signal for aliens looking for messages. Although it is unlikely that aliens could make much sense of the picture, they would recognize it as being sent by an intelligent being somewhere in space.

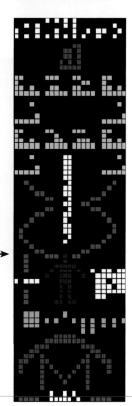

Arecibo message →

1973

The Big Ear Observatory in Ohio, USA, started looking continually for intelligent life elsewhere in the universe.

1970

1971

The first **microprocessor** was produced in the United States. A microprocessor is a tiny piece of silicon etched with electronic circuits. It can be used to store the instructions that control computers and computerized objects.

1972

The American spacecraft Mariner 9 sent the first close-up **photos of Mars** from orbit around the planet.

Salyut 1 space station

1971

The first **space station**, Salyut 1, went into orbit. Three Russian cosmonauts spent 24 days on the station.

1974

For the first time, a **barcode** was scanned in a supermarket. It was on a pack of chewing gum in the Marsh supermarket in Ohio, USA. Barcodes had been invented in 1949 by Joe Woodland, who drew one in the sand of a Miami beach, but there was no technology to make them work then.

0 36000 29145 2

1975

The invention of the **Altair 8800** sparked the personal computer revolution. This first computer needed to be built from a kit and had no screen, keyboard, or mouse. It had to be reprogrammed every time it was turned on.

ALTAIR 8800 COMPUTER

1977

Two **Voyager** craft were launched from the United States, set to fly past several planets and then head off into space beyond the solar system. They each carry a "golden record" showing where they come from and how to play the record, which has photos of Earth, greetings in many languages, natural sounds, and music. These are intended for any aliens that encounter the craft. Now just outside the solar system, there is nothing to stop them, and they could continue speeding away for thousands of years.

1976

The American spacecraft Viking 1 made the first successful **landing on Mars**.

A patient prepares for scanning in the first MRI scanner

1977

The first **MRI (magnetic resonance imaging) scanner** was used to scan a human patient in the United States. Invented in 1973, the scanner uses magnetic and radio waves to produce an image of the inside of a body. The first organism scanned with an MRI scanner was a clam, in 1973.

1979

1978

Louise Brown, the first **"test-tube baby,"** was born in the UK. The egg that grew into Louise was fertilized outside her mother's body and implanted in her mother to develop into a baby. The technique is now widely used for people who have trouble getting pregnant.

COMPUTERIZING THE WORLD

Today, it seems as though our whole lives are computerized. Hardly anything happens without a computer chip being involved somewhere. But this has come about since the middle of the twentieth century.

FIRST STEPS

Ada Lovelace

The idea of a **computer** began long ago, with Babbage's unfinished Difference Engine. This had a set of instructions, which we would now call a program, produced by Ada Lovelace. People began to put more effort into building computers in the twentieth century, starting with Konrad Zuse in Germany and the "Colossus" built to help the war effort in England. After World War II, large organizations and businesses began to install computers. These machines were vast, filling whole rooms. They did not have screens or keyboards and were programmed by connecting wires together.

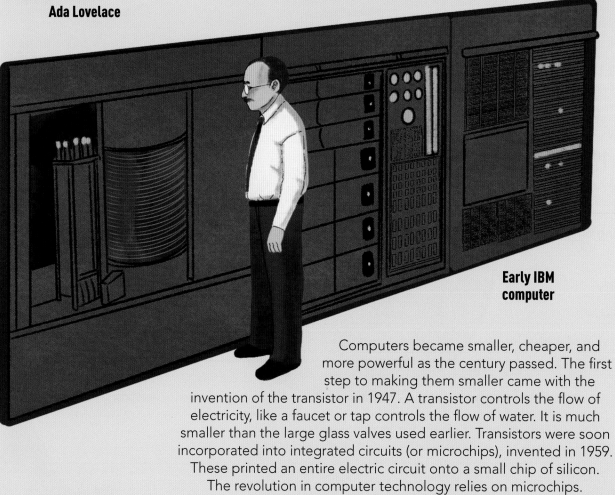

Early IBM computer

Computers became smaller, cheaper, and more powerful as the century passed. The first step to making them smaller came with the invention of the transistor in 1947. A transistor controls the flow of electricity, like a faucet or tap controls the flow of water. It is much smaller than the large glass valves used earlier. Transistors were soon incorporated into integrated circuits (or microchips), invented in 1959. These printed an entire electric circuit onto a small chip of silicon. The revolution in computer technology relies on microchips.

SHRINKING COMPUTERS

When Intel produced the first microprocessor in 1971, **personal computers** (PCs) became possible. A microprocessor combines the microchips that perform the main functions of a computer's "brain" in a tiny piece of hardware. The first attempt at a personal computer, the Kenbak-1, the first video arcade game, the first floppy disk, and the first e-book all date from 1971. By the mid-1980s, computer chips were everywhere: in watches, cars, washing machines, and an array of other things. Personal computers quickly adopted the now-familiar screen arrangement of windows, menus, and icons. This was first used on the Xerox Alto in 1973, but it became widespread with the Apple Lisa in 1983 and the first Apple Mac in 1984.

Early IBM personal computer

Xerox Alto

GETTING TOGETHER

The first computers were not connected to one another. The **Internet** developed over several years. It started with the invention of "packet switching" in 1966, which is a method of packaging data into chunks to move it around.

In 1969, computers at four sites in the United States were connected as a network to share computer processing time. This was called ARPANET.

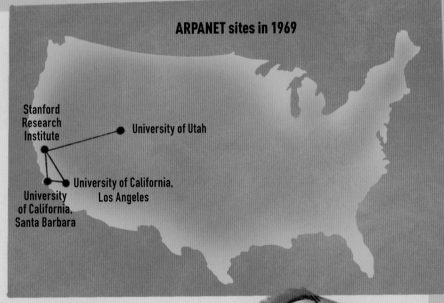

ARPANET sites in 1969

Stanford Research Institute

University of Utah

University of California, Los Angeles

University of California, Santa Barbara

The Internet is not just linked computers, it is a "network of networks." As more computers were connected to networks and cabling spread far and wide, the Internet could grow ever larger, until now it spans the globe. It even extends into space, with servers on orbiters around the Moon and Mars. For most people, the Internet became useful with the invention of the World Wide Web, allowing people to search for, connect, and share information.

Tim Berners-Lee invented the World Wide Web in 1989

1980–1989

As many countries in the world grew richer, more money was poured into science and technology. But the effects of modern life on the environment were emerging, with hints of coming climate change and the appearance of a hole in the ozone layer.

1981

The American space shuttle Columbia was launched, the first **reusable spacecraft**. It carried astronauts and objects into space.

1983

Apple launched the Lisa, the first personal computer to use a **mouse**, with windows, menus, and icons rather than a system based on typing instructions.

1980

Smallpox became the **first disease to be completely wiped out in nature** after a worldwide vaccination effort. The last case, in 1978, happened after a laboratory accident.

1980

1980

American scientists Luis and Walter Alvarez suggested that a **huge asteroid smashed into Earth** 65.5 million years ago, causing the extinction of the non-bird dinosaurs. It would have created disastrous flooding and fires immediately, with extreme climate change lasting years.

1981

The first successful **transplant of a heart and lungs** at the same time was performed in the United States. The patient lived another five years.

1984

American astronaut Bruce McCandless made an **untethered spacewalk**—a spacewalk without a cable connecting the astronaut to a spacecraft. To move around, he used a backpack with booster jets called a Manned Maneuvering Unit.

1981

IBM launched its first **personal computer** in the United States. It eventually became the standard PC used around the world.

STRETCHING THE BOUNDARIES

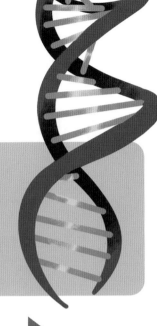

1986

A catastrophic explosion at a nuclear power station in **Chernobyl** (now in Ukraine) poured radioactive material into the atmosphere. Radiation can cause cancer, and many thousands of people were exposed to radiation. The area nearest to the reactor remains uninhabitable, since the contamination can't be cleaned away.

1986

DNA profiling was used in the UK to identify a man who was then found guilty of murder. The profiling technique had been discovered accidentally by geneticist Alec Jeffreys, who was studying inherited illness.

1985

A **hole in the ozone layer** above Antarctica was discovered. The ozone layer protects Earth's surface from damaging radiation from the Sun. From 1987, laws limited the use of chemicals that damage the ozone layer.

1989

1988

The Intergovernmental Panel on Climate Change (IPCC) was established to start a global fight to prevent disastrous warming of the planet—**"global warming"**—as a result of climate change.

1989

The first project to **map the density of the visible universe** began. The COBE (Cosmic Background Explorer) satellite mapped the microwave cosmic background radiation. This is the leftover radiation from the Big Bang and reveals which areas of the universe are denser than others.

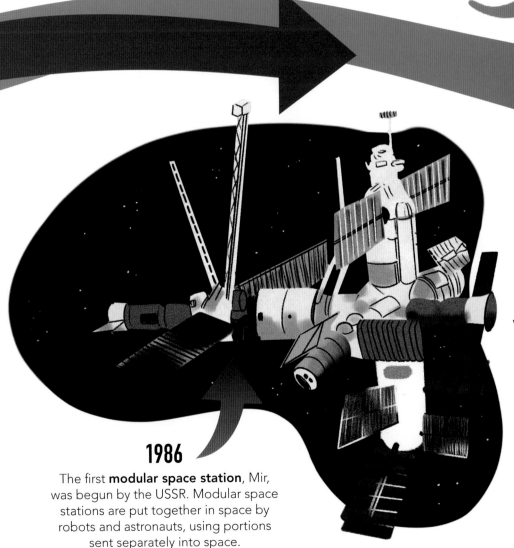

1986

The first **modular space station**, Mir, was begun by the USSR. Modular space stations are put together in space by robots and astronauts, using portions sent separately into space.

1990–1999

The 1990s saw huge developments in space science, including the astonishing discovery of dark energy, which forces the universe to grow ever faster.

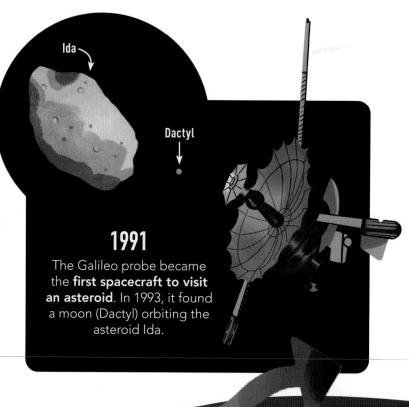

Ida

Dactyl

1991

The Galileo probe became the **first spacecraft to visit an asteroid**. In 1993, it found a moon (Dactyl) orbiting the asteroid Ida.

1991

The first **web page** was published. The first web browser, pictures on web pages, and the first webcam to feed live video followed soon afterward.

1990

The departing Voyager 1 spacecraft took the famous "pale blue dot" **photo of Earth** from a distance of 6 million km (3 ½ million miles).

1990

1991

The **Chicxulub crater** off the coast of Mexico was identified as being created by the asteroid that caused the extinction of the non-bird dinosaurs 65.5 million years ago.

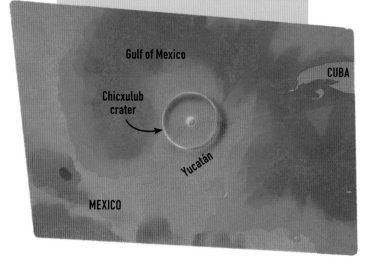

Gulf of Mexico

CUBA

Chicxulub crater

Yucatán

MEXICO

1990

The **Hubble Space Telescope** was launched to take high-quality photographs of distant objects in space. Being outside the atmosphere gives it a clear view and allows it to "see" in ultraviolet, which is blocked by the atmosphere on Earth. It has sent back hundreds of thousands of photos since its launch.

1990

The **Human Genome Project** was launched to list all the genes in the human chromosomes—the genetic material that defines us as a species and as individuals (see page 124).

1994

The Flavr Savr tomato became the first **genetically modified food** to go on sale in the United States. It had been genetically altered to keep it from rotting.

1997

The **Kyoto Protocol**, an international agreement to limit and reduce the emission of greenhouse gases that produce climate change, was agreed.

1997

The American lander Pathfinder and its rover Sojourner **landed on Mars**. Sojourner was the first spacecraft to move over the surface of another planet.

1998

Astronomers found evidence that the universe is expanding ever more quickly and that it is 13.8 billion years old. The accelerating expansion suggests there is an antigravity force working to push the universe apart. This has been called **dark energy**.

1992

Astronaut Mae Jemison became the first African American woman to travel into space. She conducted experiments on board Space Shuttle Endeavour which would help medical doctors **perform procedures during space travel**.

1992

The first **exoplanet** was discovered. An exoplanet is a planet outside our solar system that orbits a star other than the Sun.

1999

1996

The first mammal to be **cloned** from an adult cell was a sheep named Dolly, which was born in Scotland. A clone is produced by making an exact copy of an animal—it is grown from a cell taken from its body (rather than from an egg and sperm cell from two animals).

1998

The first **robot-assisted heart surgical operations** were performed in Germany and France using a surgical robot named da Vinci. Surgeons using a robot can make very fine and precise movements while a camera shows what's happening inside the body.

Dolly the sheep with Ian Wilmut, who led the project to create her

The da Vinci robot first demonstrated its skills on a plate of fruit!

WIRELESS AND SMART

The development of the World Wide Web in 1991 transformed how we use computers. We now use personal computers, tablets, and phones to stay online constantly, keeping in touch with each other and finding information instantly. Key to this change was the development of Wi-Fi, which uses radio waves to move information between computers. Wi-Fi has freed devices from the need to be plugged into a network, so they can be used anywhere while we are out and about.

WHERE ARE YOU?

GPS, or Global Positioning System, uses a network of satellites orbiting Earth to pinpoint positions on the surface. It was first developed for military use, but now we use it for everything from GPS (satnav) systems in cars to planning a run or finding a lost phone. Our devices communicate with the network of satellites to report their exact position constantly. GPS began working fully in 1993, but it was deliberately kept less accurate for nonmilitary users until 2000.

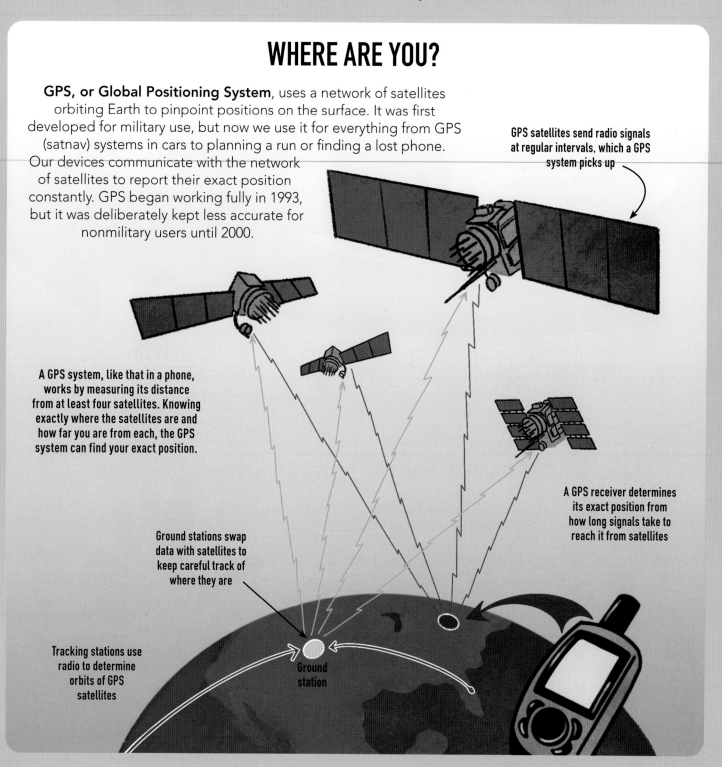

GPS satellites send radio signals at regular intervals, which a GPS system picks up

A GPS system, like that in a phone, works by measuring its distance from at least four satellites. Knowing exactly where the satellites are and how far you are from each, the GPS system can find your exact position.

A GPS receiver determines its exact position from how long signals take to reach it from satellites

Ground stations swap data with satellites to keep careful track of where they are

Tracking stations use radio to determine orbits of GPS satellites

Ground station

ALL TOGETHER

Many people use **social media** every day to keep in touch with friends and relatives, and to follow the news and their special interests. Social media relies on the posts and photos of individuals, so it could not emerge until a lot of people had a connection to the Internet, along with devices to take, share, and view photos and videos. The first social media site was Six Degrees, launched in 1997. It reached a high point of around 3 million users and set the stage for later sites such as LinkedIn (2003), MySpace (2003), Facebook (2004), Twitter (2006), and Instagram (2010).

Ordering the shopping online with a tablet computer

SMART STUFF

Widespread Wi-Fi and small, cheap computer chips have meant that many more objects can be connected **online**. This has given us things like smart thermostats that turn the heating on before people get home, smart doorbells that let us see who's at the door from a camera feed, and appliances that can learn our habits. Cameras on cyclists' helmets store video footage that can help if they have an accident.

A cyclist filming her ride with a GoPro camera attached to her helmet

A smart home can be controlled from a phone, even from a distance

ALMOST INTELLIGENT

AI (artificial intelligence) is a type of computer application that processes huge amounts of data and "learns" from its experience. The outcome of each task it deals with is fed back into the store of information to be used for the next problem. It should give more and more reliable outcomes over time. AI can be used with tasks like pattern recognition and voice recognition, so that computers can "listen" to someone's voice and understand spoken words, or they can look at images such as medical scans or data from telescopes, spotting and interpreting meaningful parts.

Some of the things most people can do easily are very difficult for a robot

2000–2009

The first decade of the twenty-first century saw new uses of Internet technology, as well as new discoveries in space and the natural world. The existence of an underground communication network between trees and plants was a shock to scientists, and changed the way we had previously thought about them.

2002

The role of underground networks of fungi, known as **mycorrhizal networks**, in enabling plants to "communicate" with and help each other became better understood. Their existence was previously known, but not their function. Through long strands of fungus, trees share and store nutrients. This helps young trees grow.

Mycorrhizal network of underground fungi attached to tree roots

2001

The first **laboratory-grown organs**, bladders, were transplanted into human patients. The new bladders were grown from the patients' own cells over a bladder-shaped scaffold and then moved into the body.

2002

The orbiter Mars 2001 Odyssey started to **map the surface of Mars**. It detected huge water-ice deposits, which suggest that Mars may once have been able to support life.

2000

2003

The first detailed **map of cosmic background microwave radiation** revealed that the universe is 13.7 billion years old.

Map of the universe showing distribution of background radiation left over from the Big Bang

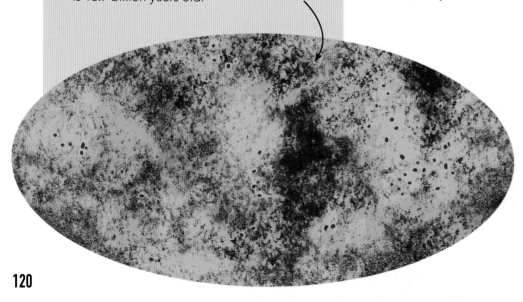

2003

The **earliest footprints of modern humans** (*Homo sapiens*) ever found were discovered in Italy and dated to 350,000 years old.

2003

A new type of early human, ***Homo floresiensis***, was discovered in Indonesia. They were much shorter than modern humans, at just 1.1 m (42 in), and have been nicknamed "hobbit." They lived 100,000 to 50,000 years ago.

2005

The first video was uploaded to **YouTube**.

2008

The brain activity of a monkey in the United States was used to control a walking robot in Japan. The monkey's **brainwaves were transferred over the Internet** to control the robot, so that the two walked at the same time and in the same way.

Monkey's thoughts control robot's legs

2009

The Pyrenean ibex became the **first extinct animal to be recreated by cloning** in Spain. The ibex lived for only seven minutes before dying.

2009

2006

The **Stardust mission** brought back dust from the comet Wild 2. This dust included an organic (carbon-containing) chemical important to life (glycine), suggesting that it was possible for the chemical ingredients of life to have come from space.

2008

The world's first **wave farm** began to harvest energy from the tide in Portugal.

2005

The galaxy VIRGOHI21 was discovered. It has no light from stars and seems to be made entirely of **dark matter** (matter that produces no light).

In a wave farm, a device on the water's surface is moved up and down by the waves, driving an electric generator

2009

The **Kepler space telescope** was launched to look for exoplanets.

2010–2019

Progress in medical treatments and discoveries about anicent lands and organisms—and even our own bodies—made for an exciting time in science. But the end of the decade was marked by the start of the global pandemic of COVID-19, which would demand much of scientists.

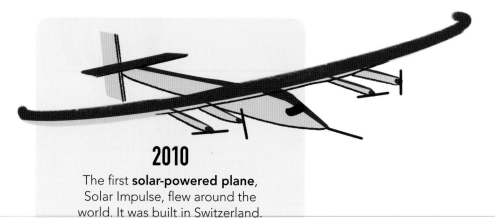

2010

The first **solar-powered plane**, Solar Impulse, flew around the world. It was built in Switzerland.

2015

The spacecraft New Horizons sent the first detailed **photos of Pluto** back to Earth.

2010

2011

Scientists calculated that there are **8.7 million species** of living things on Earth. Only around one-tenth of them have been named and described so far.

2013

The **CRISPR gene-editing technique** was developed, making precise changes in the genes of an organism much easier to achieve (see pages 125 and 127).

2013

A **pill-sized, swallowable medical camera** was tested on patients. It shows the inside of the gut and the throat, helping doctors to spot cancer, and is more comfortable for the patient than using a tube with a camera at the end.

2012

Two blind men had their **sight partially restored** by microchip implants developed in Germany. The implants do the same job that cells on the back surface of the eye do in a person with healthy eyes: They detect light falling on them and send an electrical signal to the brain, which builds the information into an image.

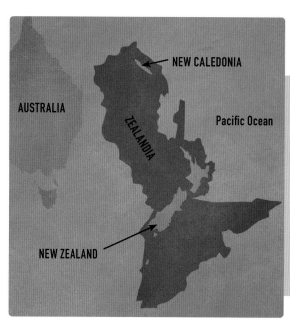

2017

An **ancient underwater continent** was discovered surrounding New Zealand. It has been called Zealandia and is about the size of Australia. The land is about one billion years old and has been completely sunk for more than 20 million years.

2018

The prehistoric Dickinsonia was confirmed as an animal. It lived 558 million years ago and is the oldest known bilateral animal (animal with two identical sides) for which we have a fossil of the body.

A new virus that causes the disease COVID-19 emerged in China in 2019. It soon gave rise to the worst global pandemic in 100 years. It spread much more quickly than previous major pandemics, as air travel carried infected people around the world in a matter of hours. By early 2022, six million people had died from the disease.

Coronavirus that causes COVID-19

2019

The Chinese spacecraft Chang'e 4 landed on the **far side of the Moon** with its rover Yutu-2 to begin studies of the side we never see from Earth.

2019

2017

The first **interstellar rock**, 'Oumuamua, was detected going through the solar system.

2018

"Zombie bacteria" that can live for millions of years were discovered miles below Earth's surface. Around 70 percent of Earth's bacteria probably live underground. Their total mass is several hundred times the total mass of humans.

2019

Astronomers took the first **photo of a black hole**.

2018

A layer previously thought of as just part of our skin was identified as a new organ called the **interstitium**. It is responsible for helping to move fluids around the body. It consists of a network of spaces within a structure of connective tissue. The spaces are filled with fluid and act as a kind of shock absorber to protect the body.

GENETIC ENGINEERING

People have been selectively breeding animals and plants for millennia without understanding how genetics works. From the middle of the twentieth century, we have understood how DNA carries the information that defines the characteristics of an organism. The results of the Human Genome Project were published in 2001, listing all the genes on the human chromosomes. Since then, we have discovered what some genes do, begun to move genes between organisms, and even change the genetic makeup of individual organisms.

LOOKING AT GENOMES

Understanding what individual genes do in an organism gives us the chance to change them and so change the organism. This is called **genetic engineering**.

Genetic engineering has many uses. We have made plants that are more nutritious or that resist drought, animal pests, or weed killers. We have engineered microorganisms to work like miniature factories—the insulin needed to treat diabetes is now grown in vats using modified bacteria.

Many more uses are emerging. We might be able to use genetic engineering to get rid of the deadly disease malaria, which is carried by mosquitoes. One plan is to replace natural mosquitoes with altered mosquitoes that either can't pass it on or can't reproduce.

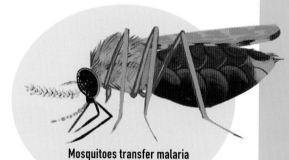

Mosquitoes transfer malaria between people

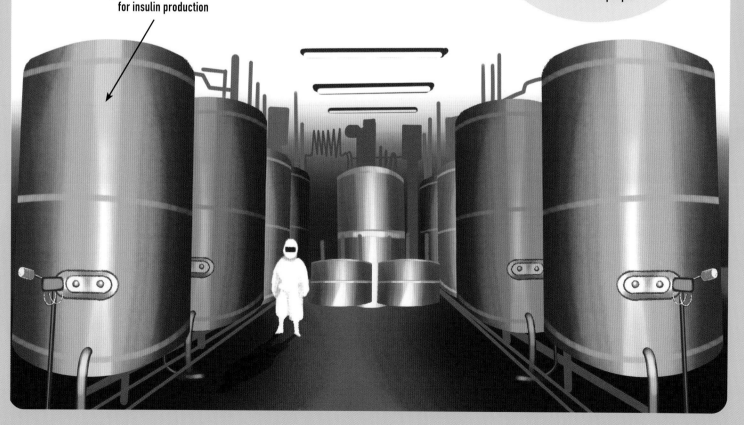

Huge vats of modified bacteria for insulin production

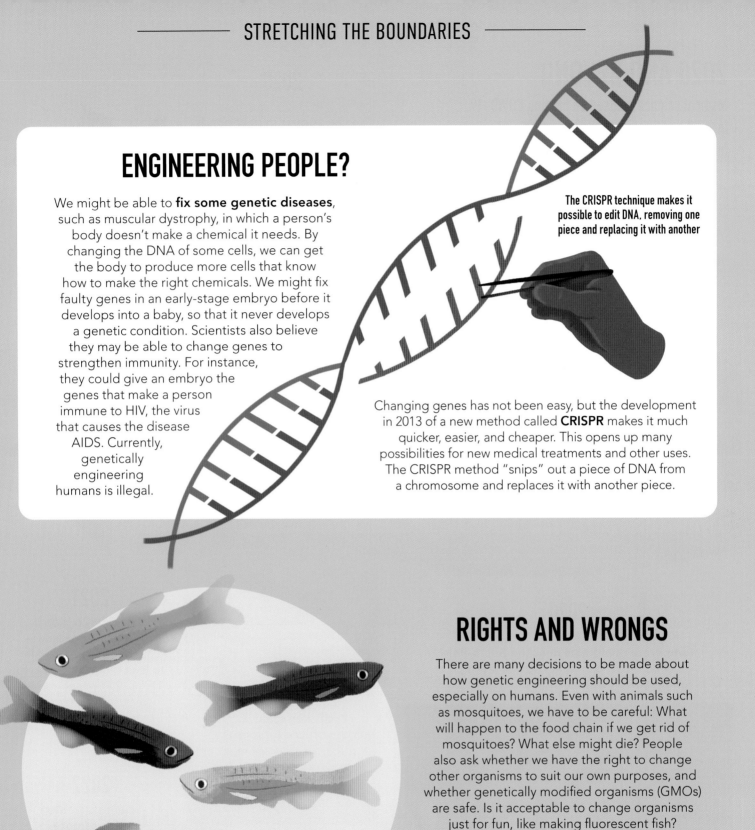

ENGINEERING PEOPLE?

We might be able to **fix some genetic diseases**, such as muscular dystrophy, in which a person's body doesn't make a chemical it needs. By changing the DNA of some cells, we can get the body to produce more cells that know how to make the right chemicals. We might fix faulty genes in an early-stage embryo before it develops into a baby, so that it never develops a genetic condition. Scientists also believe they may be able to change genes to strengthen immunity. For instance, they could give an embryo the genes that make a person immune to HIV, the virus that causes the disease AIDS. Currently, genetically engineering humans is illegal.

The CRISPR technique makes it possible to edit DNA, removing one piece and replacing it with another

Changing genes has not been easy, but the development in 2013 of a new method called **CRISPR** makes it much quicker, easier, and cheaper. This opens up many possibilities for new medical treatments and other uses. The CRISPR method "snips" out a piece of DNA from a chromosome and replaces it with another piece.

RIGHTS AND WRONGS

There are many decisions to be made about how genetic engineering should be used, especially on humans. Even with animals such as mosquitoes, we have to be careful: What will happen to the food chain if we get rid of mosquitoes? What else might die? People also ask whether we have the right to change other organisms to suit our own purposes, and whether genetically modified organisms (GMOs) are safe. Is it acceptable to change organisms just for fun, like making fluorescent fish?

Genetically engineered fluorescent fish

125

2020 AND BEYOND

Medical science focused on fighting COVID-19 in 2020 and 2021, but other sciences continued making progress as normal.

2020

The COVID-19 pandemic led to a race to produce tests, treatments, and vaccines. This saw the first use of a new type of vaccines called **mRNA vaccines**. These prompt the body to produce protein "spikes" on the outside of a virus, and the body then makes antibodies to attack the spike proteins. Since there is no exposure to the real virus, it is probably safer than other methods of vaccination.

2020

Scientists in Hungary showed that **fish can appear in new ponds**, apparently from nowhere, when birds eat fish eggs elsewhere and poop them into the water of the new pond. They then grow into fish.

1 Bird expels fish eggs eaten from a different pond

2 Fish eggs settle in new pond

3 A new fish grows

2020

The oldest *Homo erectus* skull was discovered, pushing back the date of the **first humans** to 2 million years ago.

2020

Researchers discovered that there were **temperate rainforests near the South Pole** 90 million years ago, when carbon levels and temperatures were much higher than today.

2020

Laboratory-grown chicken meat was approved for sale as food in Singapore. It was created by growing chicken cells on their own, without a chicken.

2020

Tiny particles in a meteorite that fell in Australia in 1969 were found to be 7 billion years old, much older than Earth. They must have formed **elsewhere in the universe**.

2021

The **COP26** global conference on climate change repeated an aim to limit global warming to 1.5° C (2.7° F) and reduce coal use. The target is unlikely to be met.

2022

Scientists created a **tiny remote-controlled robot**, small enough to fit through the eye of a needle. It is hoped that one day robots like this may be able to move around the human body and fix problems.

INTO THE FUTURE . . .

What will happen in the coming years? We can't be sure, but these are some things that might well happen or that scientists are working on.

SKY CROPS

Vertical farming involves growing crops on a vertical surface. This means that lots of food can be grown in a small space—an objective that will become more and more important as the world's population grows and farmland is lost to climate change.

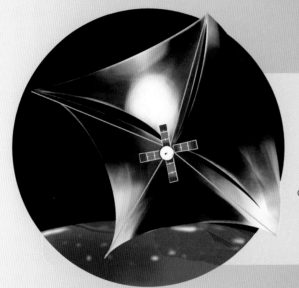

MINI-EXPLORER CRAFT

There's a plan to launch 1,000 **very small spacecraft**, just inches across, and fire them toward a planet orbiting a nearby star. Each would have a "light sail" 4 m (13 ft) square and carry a camera to send back photos. A laser fired against the sail would accelerate the craft to a very high speed. It would still take more than 100 years to get to the star.

CUTTING CARBON

The world will have to find new ways to capture and store carbon dioxide and produce **green energy** (which doesn't release climate-changing gases). One method of locking away carbon, tried in Iceland in 2016, involves pumping carbon dioxide into volcanic rock where it is locked into limestone. This happens naturally over hundreds of thousands of years, but can be forced to happen in just two years.

MOLECULAR MEDICINE

Genetic engineering using CRISPR will be used to fix more inherited conditions, and mRNA vaccines will be developed for more illnesses.

Many people dream of a colony on Mars, supported by the growth of its own food. Perhaps it will be there by 2100.

TRIP TO MARS

NASA is already planning a **human expedition to Mars**, although there are problems that can't be overcome currently. The trip would take a few years and need a lot of supplies for people to survive, but it will probably happen eventually.

INDEX